Ice Maiden

Ice Maiden

SALLY PRUE

OXFORD
UNIVERSITY PRESS

OXFORD
UNIVERSITY PRESS

Great Clarendon Street, Oxford OX2 6DP

Oxford University Press is a department of the University of Oxford.
It furthers the University's objective of excellence in research, scholarship,
and education by publishing worldwide in

Oxford New York

Auckland Cape Town Dar es Salaam Hong Kong Karachi
Kuala Lumpur Madrid Melbourne Mexico City Nairobi
New Delhi Shanghai Taipei Toronto

With offices in

Argentina Austria Brazil Chile Czech Republic France Greece
Guatemala Hungary Italy Japan Poland Portugal Singapore
South Korea Switzerland Thailand Turkey Ukraine Vietnam

Oxford is a registered trade mark of Oxford University Press
in the UK and in certain other countries

British Library Cataloguing in Publication Data

Data available

ISBN: 978-0-19-272965-1

1 3 5 7 9 10 8 6 4 2

Printed in Great Britain
Paper used in the production of this book is a natural,
recyclable product made from wood grown in sustainable forests.
The manufacturing process conforms to the environmental
regulations of the country of origin.

For Liz Cross

1

Franz was falling. He lunged out desperately, grabbed a scabby branch, and swung for one horrible moment. He was ten metres above the ground, and he was losing his grip. Any moment now—

He kicked out madly, and his foot found the stub of a broken-off branch just in time.

Franz swallowed down the sick-taste of panic and gazed wildly around. Something had just shoved him in the back—but there was no one anywhere near him. No *thing* anywhere near him, either. He was high up in a cherry tree in a deserted wood, for goodness' sake.

Franz waited, panting, until his heart had stopped thumping so hard in his chest. Above his head the mistle thrushes were making rattling calls like far-away machine guns, but round him the air hung still and dead. Not a breath of breeze. He couldn't have got hit by a wind-blown branch, then.

Not that it had felt like a branch.

Franz squinted round through the cage of the bare branches to the milky sky. Nothing, anywhere. *Definitely* nothing. So the watched-feeling that was raising the hairs on the back of his neck could only be . . .

. . . his imagination?

Yes, of course it could only be in his imagination. Anything else would be completely impossible.

The only problem with that was, of course, that something had just very nearly killed him.

A finger of air, cold as a ghost, slipped down Franz's collar and made him shudder. But that didn't mean there was anything to worry about. This was England, and there was nothing dangerous within a hundred miles. No wolves. Not even any wild boar.

Especially not up trees.

Franz forced a grin as he scanned the trees around him once more just to be certain. There were no leaves on the branches yet, so he could see quite a long way.

Nothing, except for the black branches and the lonely sky. Nothing. So unless he'd just been shoved in the back by something invisible . . .

He grinned again. This wasn't a folk tale, this was 1939. There were no fairies or elves here, any more than there were wolves. The biggest thing that could be watching him was a squirrel, and the only thing that could have just shoved him in the back was the end of a branch.

He nodded. That must be true because it was the only thing that made sense.

All right, then.

Franz took a deep calming breath and returned his attention to climbing the cherry tree. He was nearly there. Just up to that polished red limb, and then across to where the branch forked.

Franz climbed up carefully, and when he got to where he wanted to be he wedged one foot firmly into the crook of a branch. Then at last he allowed himself to look down.

But what he saw there made no more sense than anything else. Yesterday there had been four pale eggs in the mistle thrush nest.

And now there were only two.

Oh, but this really wasn't *possible*! What sort of predator would leave a nest half-robbed, for heaven's sake?

A new breath of freezing air stole round him, dropping the temperature by about ten degrees. Franz shivered. This blasted English weather! Not only that, but his watched-feeling was getting stronger with every moment, too.

The mistle thrushes were clattering alarm-calls round his head.

Franz glanced round yet again. It was impossible, completely impossible, that there could be any kind of creature anywhere near him—but he found himself tightening his hold on the branches of the cherry tree, all the same.

And at this same moment something hit him violently in the back.

He let out a yelp, just managed to stop himself falling head-first, and hastily swung himself round. The blow had come with a slash of icy air, but there was nothing behind him. Nothing at all. Nothing.

It was so utterly impossible that the next blow took him even more by surprise than the first one: a shove in his side. The sheer amazement of it was very nearly enough to make him fall backwards right out of the tree.

But there *couldn't* be anything hitting him. Because—

—another punch thudded painfully into his stomach. It left him bent forward, and then at last he did see something. There was a shining knuckle-shaped patch on the front of his coat. It was glittering with a thousand shining needles of frost.

The sight finally jolted him into action. He was ten metres up a cherry tree and he was under attack. He had to get down to the ground, fast.

He forgot all about the rules of climbing. In fact, he hardly climbed at all. He just threw himself downwards, and pretty much relied on hitting enough things on the way down to break his fall.

But his attacker, whatever it was, was coming down with him. Twice, as Franz was flinging out a hand to grab a branch, a cold fist bashed into him, pushing him off-balance and sending him slipping gut-churningly downwards.

He couldn't stop himself falling the last couple of metres. He crashed down into a gorse bush, rolled yelping away from ten thousand prickles, heard his coat rip, landed awkwardly on his hands and knees, and scrambled dizzily to his feet. But before he could get his bearings there was another waft of freezing air and a jab right at his face. It might have broken his nose if he hadn't ducked, warned by the cold of its coming.

He caught the blow on his arm, turned, and ran like a deer.

He charged between the spindly trunks of the naked

trees, his coat billowing out behind him as he went.

He could run faster once he was clear of the wood, but the wet grass was slippery and he went flying twice. Each time he rolled as he hit the ground and was on his feet again at once.

He ran right off the common and down onto the road that led to town. Even then he didn't stop: not even when he saw the fuzzy silhouettes of the alder trees that guarded the river, and the bridge over the river that led to the town. He'd been attacked by something he couldn't see, so how could he know when he was safe?

His head was so full of the invisible danger behind him that he forgot to keep an eye out for dangers ahead.

John Coker and his cronies were fishing under the bridge. The first Franz knew of them was when their heads popped up all in a row, like geese, beady-eyed and aggressive.

Franz skidded to a halt. He was a foreigner, and so of course these English boys hated him. They wanted him out of their town and out of their country, and they'd been on the look-out for a chance to get him for weeks.

John Coker hauled himself up the low wall and onto the grass. He was holding a heavy stick. The sight of it made Franz's head go crystal clear.

He threw himself across the road and down the alley that led to the South Bridge, and then he fled through the streets towards his house.

Jeering words pursued him. *Kraut! Nazi!*

They flew through the cool air and pierced his back like arrows, or flakes of sharpened ice.

* * *

His mother opened the door. Her face was pale and anxious and squirrelish, as it always was since they'd come to England.

Franz opened his mouth to tell her everything that had happened.

But then he remembered Berlin, and he didn't.

2

The sky over the common was as white as a blind eye, but above the clouds the stars were fighting.

Edrin stood watching them, glorying in their savagery, as the stars flung boiling flames of gold and scarlet across the universe.

But the weight of the world was pulling her back to the earth, and she hadn't the strength to stay with the stars for long. She let go of her hold on the realm of the stars, and in an instant the stars had faded and Edrin was visible again.

Well, at least the silly demon calf had run away, swift as a hawk-chased sparrow, so she didn't need to be invisible any more. She turned to more important matters.

The mistle thrushes screamed and dive-bombed and flapped as Edrin re-climbed the cherry tree, but of course it was no use. Edrin wrapped her legs firmly round the scarred bark and peered into the nest with fierce green eyes.

There were the last two eggs. Still safe. Good.

She reached her long fingers into the ragged nest and plucked them out.

The mistle thrushes were hysterical, now. Edrin kept a wary eye on them as she carefully pushed a thumb claw into the end of one of the eggs. Inside the yolk was veined with branches of blood.

Blood.

Delicious. She put the little egg to her white mouth and sucked.

When she had finished she let the empty eggshell fall and ran her long tongue rapturously over her lips. The egg had been sweetly fat and bloody.

She licked out the other egg and then climbed quickly and carefully down to the ground. That idiot demon calf had fallen from this tree and lived to run away, curse its heavy heart; but such a fall for her, who was one of the Tribe, might be enough to break her slender bones.

She dropped neatly down to the leafy floor of the wood, pulled her ragged shirt back round her, and looked all around. The wood stretched emptily away. No other demon or member of the Tribe in sight. Good. Those eggs had been small and she was still starving.

She seemed to be hungry all the time, these days. It was almost as if the more she ate, the greater her hunger grew. Perhaps it was because she had begun growing, lately, leaving childhood behind.

Edrin made herself still, so still that she could sense the amber sap stirring in the trees around her. Spring was on its way and in a few short weeks there would be food in plenty on the common.

But she couldn't wait for spring. She was hungry *now*. Hungrier than ever, with the sweet taste of blood still on her tongue. Hungry, *hungry*.

She listened again for the scream of a shrew or the croak

of a sour frog, but the air hung still and quiet around her except for the mournful chirruping of the mistle thrushes.

Well, at least that demon calf had run all the way off the common, galloped away in clumsy terror. Edrin grinned, showing her white fangs. That was something. With luck it would be too scared ever to return. Demons were a cursed nuisance, and that particular demon calf had been coming to the common nearly every day for months, now, rot it, disturbing her prey.

She could have wished that the demon calf had broken its neck in the fall from the cherry tree, except that a demon corpse lying about the common would cause trouble. Demons were slow and stupid, but they were dangerous to kill because they were all tied together with invisible vines. It was hard to believe, but it was true. Why, demon songs told of little else.

Demons shot the vines out of their eyes (the mere thought of it was enough to turn Edrin's stomach) and right into the flesh of other demons, capturing them for ever. That was why demons hardly ever went out alone, but trudged along in small herds. They were tied together with invisible vines. And even when demons *were* alone, their vines kept pulling at them, filling them with longing for each other and forcing them back together again.

Edrin drew back her lips in contempt. She supposed this demon longing to be with other demons must be a bit like the desire she had for food. Only stupid.

They were such disgusting things, those invisible demon vines. Two vine-tied demons would do anything for each other—share their box-houses, even share their *food*.

Mad. Disgusting. Why, the vines even kept their hold when one of the demons was dead and rotting, pulling at the live one and sending it half mad with longing and despair.

So that meant that a demon corpse on the common would attract nearly as many sad and vengeful demons as it did flies.

Edrin spat out her disgust in a long line of glistening blue saliva. Merely *touching* that demon calf had made her want to vomit. It wasn't that it was especially hideous—it was shiny-haired, and it was slender, for a demon—but it had been hot, and the beating of its great heart had rumbled like thunder, and its eyes had been searching, searching, trying to find her so that it could shoot her full of slave-vines and capture her for ever.

The thought of being bound to that thing even for a moment—

—but there! There, through the trees!

Sia. That was Sia, tall and shadowy-silver.

Sia was Edrin's kin, and one of the most powerful of their Tribe. Sia was one of the most deadly of the Tribe, too; and lately, Sia's face had become full of plans and hatred whenever Edrin was near.

Edrin slipped round to the far side of an iron-grey may tree and pulled the tails of her shirt close round her out of sight. She stilled her body and breath, pressing herself against the fine crusts of green lichen that splotched the trunk.

There were quicker ways of dying than starving to death; and meeting Sia might well be one of them.

3

If Franz's mother was a squirrel then his father was a wolf, long and grey and with a fast loping walk.

Franz and the Squirrel had come to England for a holiday, or so the Wolf and the Squirrel said (and *kept* saying, even though the Squirrel was so frightened of English people that she'd hardly set foot outside the door all through the long winter months she and Franz had been here).

Even when the Wolf managed to take time off from the business in Berlin to come over to visit them, things weren't much more holidayish. The Wolf practically always went out by himself as soon as breakfast was over, and generally stayed out until dusk. *For a walk*, he told Franz, even though he came back with clean shoes on even the most miserably damp English days.

So that was a lie.

But then Franz had known for some time that neither the Squirrel nor the Wolf was to be trusted.

The Wolf couldn't leave the business very often, but he was visiting England for a few days at the moment.

'I expect you'll be going up to the common again today, Franz,' said the Wolf, as he buttered his breakfast toast.

11

Franz nodded. His mouth was full, so he couldn't have replied even if he'd wanted to.

'Franz never seems to get tired of the common,' the Squirrel told the Wolf, rather wistfully. She hated it when Franz went out. 'Not even in this terrible English damp. He is off every day to watch the frogs or the deer. I thought he would get bored with it, but he is just as interested as ever.'

The Wolf's eyes crinkled at the corners as he looked at her. He was a wolf, but he could be as charming and smooth as a tiger.

'And I expect he always will be,' he said. 'He's been completely obsessed with animals since he was born. Do you remember that time Helga lost her mixing bowl?'

The Squirrel's anxious face suddenly broke into a smile. That was one good thing about the Wolf being in England: sometimes he could make the Squirrel forget her worries for long enough to smile.

'And Helga was no better pleased when she found it!' she exclaimed.

Franz didn't understand why his parents liked to dredge up the past in this way. The mixing bowl incident had happened several years ago. Well, he'd needed somewhere to keep his water beetles, hadn't he?

Poor old Helga had screamed the place down. Franz couldn't help smiling a little himself at the memory.

It had happened long ago, though. Long ago, when everything had been all right, and Mother and Father had been clever and loving and good, and he hadn't been completely alone.

'So, what have you found on the common, Franz?' asked the Wolf.

A thousand images shot through Franz's head. The common was stirring at last after the grey winter, and the grass was studded with blazing coltsfoot flowers. There was new life everywhere: tangles of silver-stemmed goose grass; flaunting sulphur butterflies; intricately engineered spiders; and all around the common the shouting songs of great tit, blue tit, robin, blackbird, chaffinch . . .

Franz took in a breath to speak—and then stopped. He must be careful. Neither the Wolf nor the Squirrel was to be trusted. It was difficult to remember that, sometimes. And hard, too, to be always alone.

He answered carefully.

'The tadpoles have hatched,' he said.

The Wolf grinned at him. The Wolf had sharp white teeth in his long handsome face.

'And am I likely to find anything unfortunate in the wash basin?' he asked.

Oh, it would be so easy to smile back. To share the joke.

Franz clenched his fists under the table and answered, stiffly polite.

'No, Father. I haven't brought anything back from the common.'

And he hadn't.

No.

He wouldn't be so cruel as to bring any living creature anywhere near these two.

★ ★ ★

13

Franz waited until the Wolf had left the house for his usual 'walk' and then he put on his coat. There was danger everywhere, inside as well as out, so there was no advantage in staying in. He lived with a wolf, so there was danger in the house, and being a foreigner meant there was danger in the town—and, yesterday, there had been danger on the common, too.

Although he still wasn't sure about that. He couldn't *really* have been attacked by something invisible. That was just impossible.

He'd go back today and see if he could work out what had happened. He'd look for newts in the pool, again, too. They must be coming out of hibernation any time now, and it'd be marvellous to see a newt in breeding condition, with its belly all gold and black spots.

He shouted goodbye to the Squirrel and went out.

And curse the demon calf's grey eyes but here it was back on her hunting ground again. Edrin had no idea why the wretched thing kept coming. It spent its time hunting the creatures of the common, but the great fool never, *never* managed to kill anything.

Perhaps she should have bitten its throat out while she had the chance.

She shuddered in revulsion. *Bite* a demon? Demons were full of blood, but on the whole she'd rather sink her teeth into the warts of a decaying toad.

So. What was the wretched calf doing this time? Yes, it was poking about under the cherry tree where the mistle thrush nest had been. It was after beetle grubs, perhaps. Well, she didn't begrudge it a grub or two, they made you fart like a summer stag.

Now it was heaving itself up into the branches.

The demon's limbs were short, and its body was too heavy for any but the strongest branches. Why in the name of all the stars was it climbing the cherry tree? It *knew* she'd found that nest.

But here she was, watching it again. *Again*, when the thing was hot and fat and of no use to her at all. Anyone would think it had sent its slave-vines through her flesh. Which it hadn't. It *hadn't*.

Edrin bared her white fangs in disgust and turned away to more pleasant matters. She drew her knife from her belt and neatly slit open the warm grey belly of the rabbit on her lap. The creature was thin from the long winter, but it would make the best meal she'd had for a long time.

She bit deep, gulping blissfully as its hot blood spurted into her mouth.

After a minute or two a wild waving of the branches of the cherry tree distracted her. The demon calf had found something—yes, a piece of eggshell. And now it was climbing upwards again, the great fool. As if the birds would have laid more eggs! The oaf, the *clod*!

She really wished it had died yesterday. The thing was a great nuisance—and more than a nuisance, it was a danger, too. It wasn't that it was going to spot her here amongst the soft sprouts of this honeysuckle, for demons had poor sight compared with the Tribe. But it was filling the place with great puffs of noisy breath, and she needed to be able to hear.

Edrin raised her head from the rabbit's bloody corpse and flicked an uneasy look all around. She had found this rabbit herself, sure enough. But she had found it in one of Linna's snares.

All clear.

Edrin hunched herself nearer the ground and tore fiercely at the meat with her fangs. The quicker she finished the rabbit the better: the rich metallic scent of blood was blooming into the air and any of the Tribe might sense it and come and fight her for the meat. Kill her for it, even, if it was Sia. Sia had been watching Edrin ever more closely, lately, and her glowing eyes promised violence.

But here was the demon calf again, climbing noisily and laboriously back down the tree. Ah well, Edrin supposed its smell would help mask the scent of the rabbit's blood. Yesterday she'd hardly been able to bear to go near the demon, but she'd been starving, desperate. She'd needed the rest of those mistle thrush eggs.

Edrin wiped a bloody hand stickily on a rosette of foxglove leaves. Did every member of the Tribe need so much food when it was beginning to grow out of childhood?

The demon was back down on the ground again now, gazing round with its watery eyes. Gazing right towards . . .

. . . *no, no, look away quick! Quick! Before vines grow out of its eyes and pierce you! Quick, turn your eyes away!*

Edrin flung her thin arms over her face and shrank down to the ground. The demon was staring, staring: she could feel its gaze on her skin, hot as death.

The danger, the deadly danger, was if their eyes met. Then

16

it would shoot out its slave-vines and capture her for ever and make her filled with longing whenever they were apart.

So don't look. *Don't look!*

But it was all right. It was all right. Its eyes were big and wet, but they wouldn't be able to make her out. It would think she was a glittering of raindrops, or a spangle of dew. The demon calf was useless, like all its kind. The amazing thing was that such silly slow creatures should have survived, let alone become so rich and strong.

Edrin couldn't resist a quick glance at the demon, but she was careful to keep her eyes on its ugly grey clothes and purplish knees. She was quite certain it couldn't see her—but perhaps it could *sense* her in some dim demonish way, for it spoke.

'Hello?' the demon said, uncertainly, its voice blaring and ugly. 'It's you, isn't it. I know you're there. I can feel you. Come out from the bushes!'

Edrin bared her sharp white teeth again. It was lying, she could hear it. It *didn't* know she was there.

The demon took a heavy step towards her. It was still staring and staring—*don't look into its eyes!*—but of course its gaze wasn't focused properly on her.

Its ears were glowing pink beneath its shining fawn-coloured hair.

She shrank away, revolted. She didn't know what was worst, its hoarse voice, or its great earth-shaking weight, or its musty smell.

Perhaps she should run. It would see the movement, but it would probably be too slow-witted to know what it was seeing.

But still she stayed where she was, stealing swift glances through her thin fingers. The demon was gross, ugly, nauseating ...

... but there was something about it that was fascinating all the same.

Fascinating.

Edrin squatted, entranced, as the demon peered into the bushes with its watery grey eyes.

That was why she didn't realize that Linna was close behind her until it was too late.

4

Linna's skinny arm shot over Edrin's shoulder, and suddenly the gory warmth of the rabbit had vanished from her lap.

Edrin reacted fast. She'd sprung up, turned in the air, and snatched back at the rabbit before she'd even taken breath.

She got hold of a furry leg and yanked it hard; and with a horrible elastic wrenching of skin and muscle the rabbit tore into two.

There was a moment of frozen fury. Then Linna put her head down, hissing, showing her long fangs.

'*Mine!*' she said.

Edrin showed her fangs, too, though they were puny compared with Linna's. Linna was much older than Edrin, and fully grown. Linna could tear Edrin's head off her skinny neck and sup the cool brains from her skull. And Linna just might do it, for Linna, too, would be hungry. At this time of the year nearly all the Tribe were hungry.

Linna's clawed hand struck out, a lightning swipe at Edrin's eyes: but Edrin had moved faster still, and Linna only succeeded in scything away a long straggle of white skin from Edrin's cheek.

Edrin used that instant of Linna's failure to run. She turned and fled across the clearing, and Linna sprang after her in a rush of glittering silver.

The half-rabbit, flopping twin black bulbs of juicy eyes, slowed Edrin down a little, but she couldn't afford to drop it. At this time of year even the deer were reduced to browsing on sour ivy berries and bramble leaves. The last thing Edrin had eaten were yesterday's mistle thrush eggs, and they had hardly been enough to call up her drool.

Edrin ran, hare-swift, using every ounce of muscle and strength and concentration to run and twist and swerve through the trees. Linna was stronger than she was and Edrin had no chance of out-running her; there was no time for Edrin to call on the stars to make her invisible, either. No escape that way.

Soon Edrin would have to give up the half-rabbit. She'd throw it at Linna, and Linna would snatch it and devour it at once. Linna, like Sia, had been eyeing Edrin fiercely, lately; but meat was precious, and the common was full of sharp eyes and empty bellies.

Edrin ran on while she could. If she didn't get food soon, proper substantial food and not just a clutch of tiny eggs, she'd grow weak. And then she wouldn't be able to hunt.

And then she'd starve and die.

A herd of chestnut stags threw up their heads in alarm as she pelted through the trees. If only the beasts would panic and charge across the demon road then one of them might be hit by one of the new demon chariots. Then there would be enough food for all the Tribe.

But the stags only snorted a little and turned back to nosing at the soft leaves on the ground in search of beech mast.

Edrin ran hard, ducking under licheny branches and leaping fallen boughs. She was in one of the new woods, now. This had been grassland until two dozen years ago a great herd of demons, all dressed alike in hideous brown, had tramped heavily up to the common.

And begun *digging*.

That demon herd had dug great holes, each deeper than a demon was tall. They'd dug for weeks, until the whole place had looked as if it'd been invaded by giant moles.

Edrin ducked under a low birch branch. She felt her shirt catch and rip, but she tore herself free and ran on.

And then one morning the demons had all marched away again, blowing their glittering painful trumpets and even more bound together with invisible slave-vines than before.

Madness. But then, demons *were* mad. It was the only explanation for their behaviour.

Edrin ran on, the half-rabbit jerking and flapping in her hand. She knew this part of the common well, every bump and hollow of it, even though the years had filled the demon pits with jutting trees and curling bracken. For of course the wilds had begun to creep back the moment the digging stopped. First tiny spikes of mauve-tinged blackthorn had sprouted from the jumbled earth; then wicked rose-loops; then holly saplings with leaves as glossy as bottles; all of them rushing to pierce the sun.

And with them came creatures: shrill shrews, juicy hedgepigs, armoured bugs.

Edrin's back was shrinking away from the vicious coldness behind her. Linna was very close, now.

Edrin swerved to avoid a pit. It was a good thing she knew this part of the common so well, because the new growth made the pits hard to see, and a fall into one of them . . .

Edrin grinned as she sped through the trees.

A fall into one of the pits.

Yes, that would do it. Now, *now!*

Edrin grabbed a springy birch branch as she charged past, ran on three steps, and let it whip back. A yelp and a curse from behind her sent a sharp shaft of triumph through her chest.

Good!

Edrin jumped round. Linna, blinded with frozen tears, was clutching at her face where the birch had lashed her.

Edrin lunged back and shoved Linna hard with both hands.

The demon-dug hole behind Linna wasn't very deep, but it was deep enough.

And Edrin was yards away before Linna hit the bottom.

5

Franz, startled, gazed across the shivering grass of the clearing. Something like a bullet of glitter had just streaked past him, but it had been out of sight before he'd had time to work out what it was. One moment he'd been peering into the shadows of a tangle of honeysuckle, and the next there'd been a gust of chilly sparkling air . . .

. . . and then nothing.

He'd only caught just a fleeting glimpse of whatever it had been, but on the whole he'd been left with an impression of running figures and glittering ribbons and flying fair hair.

Which was quite *quite* impossible.

Well, whatever it had been was gone now, and he was quite alone again. Franz shrugged, went back to the cherry tree, and finished fitting the pieces of mistle thrush eggshell together. Yes, there were four eggshells here. The whole clutch.

But what had taken them? It might have been magpies, or the strange grey English squirrels.

Except that yesterday he'd felt that waft of cold air and the shove of that icy hand. And today . . .

'Perhaps Franz should stay in the house where it is safe,'

the Squirrel had said, last night, when the tear in his coat had forced Franz to admit that he'd fallen out of a tree.

'What?' the Wolf had said, incredulously. 'Where it's *safe*? But this is England, Brunhilda. It's all safe.'

Franz's mother had raised her hands to her throat in a pathetic, squirrelish gesture.

'But Alex—'

'Quite safe,' the Wolf had repeated, firmly. 'You know that, don't you. No wild boar. No bears. Not even an ogre or an ice maiden!'

'An ice maiden?' Franz had echoed, remembering the frosty hand-print on his coat.

His father had turned his pale wolf-eyes on him, a little surprised.

'Have you not heard about the ice maiden, Franz?' he'd asked. 'It's one of your typical jolly Germanic folk tales, about fifty pages long and full of doom and death. I had to study it at school. It's about a boy who keeps coming across the dreaded ice maiden whenever he goes climbing.'

'That's right,' the Squirrel had said, shuddering. 'I studied "The Ice Maiden" at school also. It is horrible.'

'What's she like?' Franz had asked her.

'Oh, she is something like a ghoul,' the Squirrel had said. 'Very cold. With long white hair.'

'Who likes nothing better than to lure people to her palace and then kiss them dead,' the Wolf had gone on, cheerfully. 'Of course she gets the boy in the end. He drowns, I think.'

A shiver of doubt had run down Franz's spine. Someone *cold*. But the Wolf had only given a hoot of laughter at the look on his face.

'You're as bad as your mother,' he'd said. 'This is nineteen thirty-nine. All the ghosts and fairies are long gone.' Then the Wolf frowned, and went on: 'I say, your imagination hasn't been playing you tricks again, has it, Franz?'

The Wolf had developed a habit of blaming things on Franz's imagination. That was mostly because of the spiders. Not ordinary spiders, of course, Franz didn't mind them: in fact he was fascinated by the spiders of the common. They were everywhere—yes, there was one right in front of him now, on that branch: a thin golden one, with hunched reaching-forward forelegs.

No, the spiders that caused the trouble were huge things half as tall as Franz. They hunted him nearly every night. Black, angular, four-legged spiders. Franz, cornered, would look into their hungry black eyes, and all he could do—*all* he could do—was scream in utter despairing terror.

But then the next moment the Squirrel would be peering white-faced round his bedroom door saying, *It's only a dream. It's all right, Franz. It's all right, my love, it's only a dream.*

And of course she was right. This was England and it was only a dream.

A movement caught Franz's eye amongst the papery leaf-litter of the common. It was an ant, very elegant, and as black and shiny as a soldier's boots. It was clambering doggedly along the wavy edge of an oak leaf.

And there was another one. Franz moved his hand hastily, because it was sniffing (sniffing?) at his finger. Did these English ants bite?

25

If the ant had crawled up onto his hand, where would it have thought it was? Suppose it had crawled over the pits and furrows of his skin to the skating-rink of his nail and then back to its home, what would it have told the others? That it'd found a place where the ice was warm? Where the ground could pick itself up and move through the air at impossible speeds?

And what would the old stay-at-home ants have said when they heard?

Imagination, most probably.

Franz sighed, gently, so as not to disturb the ant. Now he looked closely he was discovering there were ants all over the place, all off on some expedition (To hunt for food? For water? To attack other sorts of ants? How could he know?). They were all hurrying along, intent, business-like. Like the soldiers that marched along the streets of Berlin under the spider-stamped flags.

Only a dream, the Squirrel said when Franz dreamt of huge spiders. But could something be *only* a dream? Could dreams sprout from the air, or did they have to have something to start them off, something to grow on?

Because Franz's dreams were not *only* dreams, he was sure of that. The reality that had seeded them was muddled up in his mind with horror and memory and midnight, but there had certainly been black shiny soldiers' boots marching along the streets that last night in Berlin. They'd tramped into his dreams and woken him up to the starchy smell of fine Berlin bed-linen.

Then, later, there'd been whole crowds out in the street—he'd heard them shouting—and then there'd been running footsteps, and glass smashing. Cheers. Then more glass. And then more, quite close.

Screams.

Franz wished he could remember it all properly. He'd gone to the window and looked out. (Or had that bit been *really* only a dream?) There'd been a many-tentacled shadow outside, studded with pale faces; and then a herd of terrible four-legged spiders had begun climbing up the walls to his room. (Which *must* be a dream. Of course it must.)

In any case, he'd certainly been asleep at some point because he'd been awoken by a huge crash that had sent the curtains gusting wildly, and flickering fragments of glass pattering all over his bed.

He'd sat up in shock. Opened his mouth to call for help.

But he'd never actually made a sound, because downstairs someone was battering on the front door. So he'd got up quietly and gone to peer out onto the landing. But everything must have been all right, after all, because someone was opening the front door to let the people in.

And then it was somehow morning, and the Squirrel was coming in all in a hurry to pack for this sudden surprise holiday to England.

And here they were. In England.

And the spiders . . .

The thing was, the spiders stalked through so many of Franz's memories of Berlin that he couldn't honestly be sure exactly what was real. The spiders were even mixed up in Franz's mind with the bright parades of motor cars, and with those other days when he'd been coming home from school and seen—

Franz took a deep breath.

He didn't want to remember some of the things he'd seen on the streets of Berlin.

Berlin was his home, though, all the same. And it had been quite ordinary most of the time. There'd been school, the park, shopping. The zoo. Parties.

Yes, lots of grown-up evening parties, with the Squirrel in a shiny long gown, and the Wolf sleek in black and white, and much laughter from behind closed downstairs doors. Important parties for important people, because the Squirrel and the Wolf were members of the Nazi Party and had many powerful friends.

Franz had looked down from his bedroom window on party nights at the cars and their chauffeurs, waiting in the street outside. Long-nosed cars, and men quietly smoking, four-legged spiders stamped on their brown arms.

And inside, down the stairs, loud laughter from behind closed doors.

6

There was a *thump* as Linna hit the bottom of the demon hole, and then a *crack!*

Edrin didn't stop. She pelted through the skinny young trees until she came to an oak, gnarled and ancient, which had been only an acorn when she was calved. She climbed it easily, the half-rabbit held between her teeth. She found a place to perch and then she devoured the half-rabbit, scraping the meat down to the skin with her sharp incisors.

The rabbit's fur was warm and fine. When she blew on the cloud-grey pelt it parted to reveal a fluffy whiteness, fine as thistledown.

The pelt was lovely, but no use: it would rot and moult in days. Only demons, who knew ways to steep the skin in piss and foulness, made fur that lasted.

Edrin let the thing drop and lay back to digest her meal.

It wasn't long before there was a movement in the leaves below her, but it was only the Tribe-infant. The silly creature was too young to climb, or even walk, but he had sniffed out the pelt. He grabbed it with a small fist and crammed as much as it could into his mouth. Edrin had stripped the meat away, but the infant would get a taste of blood from it. It would make a change for him from earwigs, anyway.

It was not long now until dusk. Edrin would go and hide in the ivy-clad ash tree where the starlings roosted and see if she could snatch one or two as they came in to rest.

She ran her tongue over her lips, imagining the bird's fragile bones crunching in her mouth. Her hunger was stirring again already, although she'd just eaten, She wanted more, *needed* more food. Needed it with a greed and a passion. Sometimes she wondered if there was any creature on the common big enough to satisfy her hunger. Well, she hadn't the strength to kill a deer. The next meatiest thing on the common was the demon calf, but she dismissed its image from her mind. She'd rather sup on a fox's turd than a demon.

But halfway to the starling roost a voice halted her. A high, cold voice. Not the voice of the wind, or an animal, or a star. A Tribe voice.

She froze, instantly alert. The people of the Tribe sang, but they seldom spoke. They spoke only at some great need.

What great need?

She stole through the trees with the utmost care.

'*Curse you!*'

That was Linna's voice. It sounded as if she was still in the pit.

Why?

Edrin put out an ivory arm and pulled herself up into a birch tree so she could see.

'Your leg is broken.'

Larn. That was Larn's voice. Yes, and Sia was with him, too. Larn was strong and beautiful, a skilled hunter, silver-speared and full grown. He was the most dangerous of all the Tribe, and he, like Sia, had been watching Edrin lately.

'Linna will die, then,' said Sia.

Edrin moved her head a little, and in her new splinter of vision she saw a sparkle of silver as Sia leapt down into the pit where Linna lay.

'May your hunting fail always!' Linna spat.

Sia only stayed in the pit for a moment. She came out clutching something which spat gleams of light into the dimness between the unclothed trees.

Sia held it up to the sky, admiring its sheen and music. Linna's silver chain.

But why had Linna let Sia take it? The Tribe would generally fight to the death over silver.

Sia had turned away, now, and was walking off through the wood.

Larn was turning away from the pit, too. His white lips were stained dark. Yes, one last leg of Linna's half of the rabbit swung from his hand.

But there was no sound or sign of movement from Linna.

When silence had re-emerged into the wood, Edrin came down from her tree and continued quietly on her way to the starling roost. Sia was right. If Linna's leg was broken then she would certainly be dead very soon, for she would not be able to hunt. Not that Linna would wait to die. She had her knife. If Sia had left her alive then Linna would choose to join the stars at once.

Which was good. That meant Linna's territory would

be free. Edrin would be able to take over Linna's snares.

Edrin passed quite close to the demon calf, who was peering at a colony of ants. (Which were so acrid that no creature save the laughing woodpecker could eat them. What a great clod the demon was, what an *oaf*.) The demon's sight was so poor that it did not notice her, even though she walked past it in plain sight.

But it shivered and got up. Then it pulled its heavy coat more closely round it, and began to trudge back down towards the demon road.

7

Edrin waited until the sky was dark before she climbed angrily down from the ash tree. The smoke-like swarms of starlings had not come. The winter had passed, and the spring had called them away to mate and nest, and Edrin could hunt no more starlings until leaf-fall.

Edrin prowled the common, senses alert for food. She found a hedgepig carcass under a heap of logs, but the maggots had had most of it and it didn't even begin to take the edge off her hunger.

Her best chance of food was if Larn killed a deer. That was almost the only time the Tribe came together, when there was so much meat that all could gorge and there was no use in fighting.

But Larn was so strong that he hardly needed to eat from one week's end to the next. Edrin needed to eat all the time. *All* the time. She needed to eat *now*.

She prowled on. She had to concentrate completely, ready to pounce on every mouse-rustle or shrew-squeak. It was infuriating, because somehow the image of the demon calf had somehow burrowed itself into her mind and kept teasing her with its fatness.

She went round Linna's snares, but they were all empty, curse her bones.

And there was a thought.

Linna's bones?

Edrin crammed the tail of a still-wriggling slow-worm into her mouth and made her way back through the darkness to the demon pits. There was no sign of movement anywhere, except for the shivering of the pale-backed bramble leaves. Edrin inched carefully towards the edge of Linna's pit, nose twitching, searching.

All she could see . . .

Yes! Edrin bared her gleaming fangs in triumph. It was just as she'd hoped. Sia had taken Linna's silver chain, but she'd not touched her gown. It lay glittering in the moonlight, draped over the ridges of Linna's bones. A few hours had seen the whole skeleton picked quite clean of meat. The weasels and foxes and beetles had done their work well. Good.

Edrin tugged the shimmering gown free of the skeleton. Linna's spine and some of the other bones were still holding together, but once the sun found its way into this hollow the bones would melt in the heat and that would be the end of her.

Edrin shrugged herself out of her shirt. It was an old, thin, ugly thing, but it had been all she could find, for even demons, who had so many possessions, seldom discarded garments on the common.

It was different for Sia, who was strong. Sia could stay invisible for hours. She could go right into the demon city and steal whatever she wanted: bottles of demon wine, hunks of meat, gowns of shimmering silver, chiming silver chains.

Edrin tore her shirt contemptuously to rags and shoved it into the mouth of an old badger sett. Then she slipped Linna's gown, heavy with sequins, over her head.

The gown was too long for her, but it would soon tear itself shorter. Edrin looked down at herself, marvelling, as the moon came out from behind a cloud and slid its fingers over her. She had grown, lately—and, she realized with amazement, not only upwards. She stroked her hands wonderingly over the gown's shining silver curves.

For a moment Edrin found herself almost admiring the demons who could make such stuff.

Edrin had never dared go to the demon city, but it was said the place held riches beyond counting. She could believe it. The demons that came to the common were fat and well-clothed. Demons had boots, coats, mirrors. They'd even found a way to make chariots that rode through the air: Edrin had seen them, churring overhead like silver nightjars.

Perhaps one day the demons would reach the realm of the stars, and then all the Tribe would be caught and enslaved. Yes, even Larn with his strong spear arm. Even Sia, so filled with cruelty and power.

It was strange to think that a clod like the demon calf could make such wonderful things. That a demon might be more powerful in some ways even than Larn or Sia.

Not that the calf would have a chance against either of them if it came to a fight. The calf was immensely strong, but very slow. Larn could stab it before it knew he was there, and the thing's thick blood would fountain richly into the air.

Oh, she was so *hungry*!

She stilled her bones and listened carefully. Nothing. Not even the chattering of a shaggy vole.

No food here, unless she dug into a stinging ants' nest for a handful of grubs, or paddled into the cold pool after a frog.

Once more a vision of that solitary demon calf stole into Edrin's mind. Heavy, fawn-haired, wool-clothed, alone.

And as she thought of him her hunger twisted in her belly more fiercely still; and suddenly her shining dress seemed to lie as cold as ice over her bones.

8

Franz had learned to be wary whenever he went out into the town. He was as much English as German, of course, because the Wolf was English; but as far as the people of this town were concerned everything about Franz was foreign, and slightly wrong.

His English was too grammatical, for a start. And then he was too polite in some ways, and sometimes rude in others. For instance, English people said *please* and *thank you* all the time, even for quite ordinary things like passing the salt.

On the other hand, snapping to attention when you were introduced to people unnerved them. Clicking your heels was even worse. It made people desperate to laugh— though they seldom did, merely going purple and giving the impression they were about to explode.

Franz's coat was wrong, too. All the other boys in the town had navy blue raincoats with dangling belts, but Franz's coat was grey and woollen and had only one row of buttons.

Franz had asked the Wolf about getting a raincoat, but the Wolf had said that it wasn't worth buying a new coat just for a holiday.

A holiday. Oh yes. There was nothing like a winter in a damp and chilly English town where everyone hated you for a hilarious time.

Franz closed the house door quietly behind him and made his lonely way through the damp morning town towards the river and the common. One part of his brain was certain that the icy fist that had pushed him out of the cherry tree the other day must have been his imagination. But in spite of that he was still going to carry on keeping a look-out for . . . well, for what he'd found himself thinking of as the ice maiden. And, after all, he had seen *something* yesterday. Something that had looked a bit like a girl—well, two girls, to be quite honest—but that was getting ridiculous.

Franz trudged past the inn that stood near the bridge over the river. It was called The Fox and Hounds. All inns in England had odd names: some were even called after bits of things, like the Saracen's Head.

He did his best not to take any notice of the twitching net curtains in the window, or the sharp English eyes that followed him all the way across the bridge.

The people of this town wanted him gone. He knew that. If John Coker and his cronies didn't get rid of him, then sooner or later someone else would. He was sure of it.

But look, there was a kestrel. Its banded tail was quivering against the wind but its head was still, searching . . .

. . . and . . .

. . . *there!*

Down, sliding swiftly, talons outstretched, striking,

killing, bouncing onto the ground. *Fantastic.* Its prey might be a whiskery-nosed shrew, perhaps, which might in its turn have been hunting for shining beetles, which might have been searching for green-jelly aphids. And now the kestrel was on the ground it might itself be the prey of a pouncing fox.

Franz went on again, full of a sort of joy at the miracle of it all. At how every creature on the common fitted into its place. How it all worked. How all the animals knew how to hunt, fight, kill, protect their territory, survive.

John Coker and his cronies had been fishing under the bridge again yesterday afternoon. They'd pelted him with lumps of mud. They never let him past unnoticed, even if they only stared at him, like bullocks about to charge, or did goose steps and *Heil Hitler* salutes or shouted *Kraut!*

But of course they were bound to hate him. Franz was on their territory, was foreign. His parents were Nazis. Here in England Franz was an outsider, just like a Jew or a Gypsy was in Berlin.

Franz shivered, remembering what happened to outsiders. He'd seen it, walking along the Berlin streets with the Squirrel and the Wolf.

That last time he'd seen kind old Frau Rosen. She'd been kneeling on the pavement with an excited, noisy crowd all round her. Franz hadn't been able to see just what she was doing, and the Squirrel and the Wolf had only laughed pleasantly and chivvied him on.

'Oh, that's nothing to worry about,' the Wolf had said, easily. (But how could it be nothing to worry about when Frau Rosen was on her hands and knees, and none of those

39

people were helping her? How? *How?*)

Or the time they'd seen a family of frightened Gypsies being escorted along the road by smartly-stepping soldiers.

'They're grown-up matters,' the Squirrel had explained, smiling reassuringly, with an elegant feather bouncing over her tiny hat. 'You're too young to understand it yet, darling.'

Well, Franz understood it now. The common had shown him the same thing again and again. People were animals, and if they were going to survive they had to defend their hunting territory. So they had to get rid of outsiders.

Franz walked on up the road. The common would be grey and damp and deserted, but at the same time it would be full, crowded, bursting with life. Even if there were no ice maiden, Franz would only have to look for a minute to find some other marvel: some creature with its marvellously jointed skeleton on the outside of its body, or with its wings covered in an intricate mosaic of tiles.

Or a melt-eyed doe, or a float-tailed squirrel.

The common beckoned him.

9

There was a pool on the common between the trees. Franz had spent a lot of time there, crouched amongst the fluffy disintegrating dusters of the bulrushes. The pool was only a dip in the ground where the rain had collected, but the muddy edges showed prints well. Looking for something pretty much invisible (and impossible) was of course almost hopeless; but perhaps there might be tracks . . .

The water of the pond was still, and showed a perfect reflection of the wood. There were clumps of old frog spawn in the shallows, clotting the surface like miniature mudflats. Franz had watched this pond, fascinated, for hours at a time. He'd seen the frogs arrive, and then the days of manic pop-eyed mating when sometimes they launched themselves onto kicking balls of half a dozen others.

And then there'd been the spawn. First motionless, then busy with the squirming commas of the tadpoles; until now the tadpoles had thrashed their way out of their jelly prisons and disappeared into the murk.

The frogs had mostly gone, now, too.

It all worked so perfectly. Some instruction of Nature brought all the frogs here at the same time so they could mate. Because all animals (*all* animals) had to act as Nature told them. Mate, hunt, fight, kill. That was just how it had to be, or everything would fall to pieces.

Franz went to lie down on his stomach so he could see better, but then he remembered the Squirrel's clothes-washing troubles (England was cold and damp practically all the time) and thoughtfully took off his coat. He hung it from a handy branch. He even rolled up the sleeve of his jumper before he plunged his arm into the water in search of tadpoles.

It was a mild day, but the water was freezing. No wonder the frogs had left as soon as they could. Whole bands of them, there must have been, making their jerky way through the leaf litter in search of slugs and beetles.

There had been frog-brown groups that had marched about through Berlin, too, and they also had been searching for prey. But of course they had. The people of Berlin were animals just like the frogs. And they needed to survive. Didn't they?

Frogs, wolves and people, German and English and Slavs. They were all animals. Just as he was himself. All bound to do as Nature instructed them.

He shivered, and in front of his eyes the dream-world of the pool's reflection shivered too, as if in sympathy.

The water was too cold to feel for tadpoles. Franz sat up and flicked the water off his arm. He needed a fishing net. Perhaps if the Squirrel had a laddered stocking . . .

. . . Franz shrugged, and looked round for his coat, which he'd hung up so carefully.

But it was gone.

10

Franz turned right round twice, unable to believe it. His coat couldn't have just *vanished*. It must have fallen on the ground—blown away—got tangled up somewhere.

He was completing his second turn when a twig snapped just behind him.

Franz spun round. There was nothing to see, but a blast of cold hit him in the face, chilling his eyes.

He found himself filled with a sudden terror, but he was filled with anger, too.

'Give it back!' he said, as fiercely as he could. 'I know you're there. Give me back my coat!'

But his words only echoed back flatly from the silent trees.

Franz stared round. He couldn't see anything, but she was here, all the same. He was sure of it. The ice maiden, or whatever she was, was here. The place was filled with the same cold he'd felt when she'd attacked him in the cherry tree.

For a moment he didn't know whether to stay or run: but then he remembered the frog-brown bands of men in Berlin and he remembered that it was better to be the hunter than the hunted.

He took a step forward towards the cold. And then another, peering hard for some glimpse of a body, a face, a hand.

Nothing. And nothing. And—

—*snick!*

There, there, out of the corner of his eye, a twig shifting and breaking as if under an invisible foot.

He threw himself towards it.

'Give it to me!' he shouted. But his flailing arms found only a waft of warmer air.

He halted, baffled. The soft wind breathed against his face, but apart from that nothing was moving . . .

. . . except, except, that patch of mud! It was squashing itself down to form a footprint. And there was another one. Something was moving stealthily away from him. Yes, there were the toes, it was edging away backwards.

Franz lunged towards it. He touched something, very nearly caught hold of it, something cold like ice but dry and somehow living. His fingers even brushed against a piece of rough cloth which must be his coat.

But at once there was a whisk of icy air and the thing had turned and run—and Franz was chasing after it.

It left a stream of cold air in its wake which he could have followed, even if here the ground hadn't been covered in papery oak leaves which scattered under its feet.

It ran fast, but Franz charged after it as best he could. He must have a chance of catching it. It was carrying his coat, which would hamper it. Perhaps it might stumble.

Watch out, watch out! It had changed direction. Franz wouldn't have realized except that something—his coat, probably—had got caught on a fallen branch and sent it vibrating like a rattle. Franz hurdled the branch and charged on.

And then suddenly, suddenly, something was flying up at his face.

He ducked violently and the thing whizzed past his ear and fell far behind him with a leaf-scattering thud. It was a stone, probably, by the sound of it—but Franz had no time to stop to look.

He half knew he was running into danger, but his senses were at full stretch keeping track of the thing and there wasn't time to work out what he should be doing. He ran on, one arm held ready to fend off any more stones.

But the next one got him anyway. He never really saw it. He just caught a glimpse of something from over to his left and the next moment something hit him hard on the side of the face.

Franz wiped the sting away and ran on. The thing had changed direction again: it had turned up that track towards the edge of the trees. He wouldn't have known, except for the trajectory of the stone.

He half-wondered where it was leading him—but there was no time to do anything but run.

Wherever it was going, he was going to do everything he possibly could to catch it.

11

The thing had led Franz right into a tract of ancient forest, now, where the great beech limbs reached upwards above trunks like boiling iron. The beech mast that covered the ground was scattering in fast little spurts in front of him, and just once he thought he heard the thing's panting breath. The freezing air it trailed was thin, but at least now Franz was so close behind it he didn't have to worry about it throwing stones any more. It didn't have time to stop to pick anything up.

And now they were out of the beech wood and into a field of young trees and bracken criss-crossed with deer paths. It was even easier to track the thing here because the old bracken shivered softly with the draught of its passing. It was only a couple of metres ahead, now.

And then a hanging curtain of birch twigs was bursting apart in front of him and just for a moment Franz got a glimpse of the shape of the thing. Head, shoulders, arms held wide like a hurdler's. It was slight (and *female*, though there was no time to work out how he knew) and moving fast. Franz held up an arm to shield his head as he charged through the swinging twigs—

—and found himself on the edge of a pit.

He was moving too fast to stop. He fell head-first, but he managed to flip himself over so he landed with a great grunting thump on his back.

He lay there for a moment, heaving in air, full of anger at his simple-mindedness. The girl—the ice maiden—had lured him here, let him get close, and then led him blind right to the edge of a pit.

The place was filled with undergrowth, so at least he'd had a softer landing than he might have done. There were about a hundred bits of twig trying to pierce holes in him, but at least he hadn't broken his back. He tugged himself free from all the snagging thorns—even the *leaves* of the brambles in this pit were barbed—and sat up. He was more exasperated than anything else. By now the ice maiden would be far away, and of course his coat would have gone with her.

'Hey!' he shouted, more in anger than hope. 'All right, you tricked me! Tell me where you are!'

A little way away a crow cawed, but that only made the greater silence of the wood settle around him even more deeply.

'Hey!' he called again. 'I just want my coat back, all right? I'll be in trouble if I don't have it.'

He pushed himself to his feet and turned round, slowly, searching for a draught of chilly air. Halfway round his shoe got caught up in something. He glanced down—

—and froze.

Because under his foot, twisted through the hooked thorns of a briar, was a skeleton.

Yes. It was, it really was. There was the skull, and the cage of the ribs, and the long thigh bones.

One of the legs ... yes, it was broken. Look, there were the jagged ends.

Franz, holding his breath, bent his head as near as he dared.

The bones were white, almost glowing in the gloom of the grey spring sky.

Fine, delicate, white ...

... and, as far as Franz could tell, very *very* much like those of a human.

12

Franz stared at the skeleton which lay at his feet on the floor of the pit. He was frozen with amazement and excitement and curiosity and horror.

After a little while he put out a finger to touch the skull—but then he noticed the eye teeth, which were long and curved like a wolf's, and he hesitated.

What sort of a creature had this been? The skull was round, and the hollow eye sockets faced forward. There was no muzzle. The little bones of the hands lay scattered, but plainly they had been hands, not hooves. This *must* be human, except . . .

It was so strange he had to touch it. He had to touch it to be sure it was real.

He cautiously dabbed a finger onto the fungus-whiteness of the skull. The skull was cold, colder than even bone in damp and shadow should be. Not only that, it felt . . .

. . . odd. Wrong. Almost as if . . . almost as if the cold bone had somehow squirmed away from his finger.

And what was that white stuff underneath it?

It was a thick hank of hair. There was something else

there, too, something gleaming warm against the dead white. Yes, the hair had been caught back in a golden clasp. It was enamelled with a vivid star-pattern in the richest possible blue.

Franz stood quite still, bent over the delicate pattern of the bones. He stared and stared, still unable quite to believe it.

So he put out his finger and prodded it against the bone of the skull again.

This time there was no doubt: the white bone moved. More than that, it gave way, swiftly, bewilderingly, and before he could stop it his finger had gone right through the bone into the brain cavity.

He snatched his hand back in horror, but somehow, horribly, the whole skull came with it. Panicking, he tried to bat the thing off with his other hand, but those fingers sank into the stickily melting bone of the skull, too.

And suddenly Franz's head was full of savage laughter, and glowing eyes, and dangerous darkness.

And singing.

> *We will not tell whose men we are*
> *Nor whose men that we be.*
> *But we will hunt here in this chase*
> *In spite of thine or thee . . .*

The skull was melting. It was coating his hands with a burning slime, giving off a thick curling vapour that stung his lungs.

Franz panicked completely. He flung the decaying skull violently away from him. It flew upwards, spinning, until

50

it hung for a moment against the charcoal clouds like a dreadful moon, glaring down at him through hollow eyes.

We will hunt here in this chase.

Amidst the silence of the wood the fierce words stabbed themselves through Franz's skin.

Franz threw himself out of the way of the falling skull, grabbing and scrabbling at the side of the pit until he was up on level ground again. And then he ran, charging between the trees, slipping, tripping, anything to get out of there and away, away.

We will hunt here in this chase.

And it seemed as though the sound of the song was coming, not through the air, but through the shivering, reaching branches of the trees, and the unfurling bracken, and the circling clouds.

Even when his feet reached the road the song followed him, cold in his bones.

Hunt, hunt, hunt . . .

Down by the river, three figures detached themselves from the dimness under the bridge. They climbed the grassy bank and came towards Franz.

But there was so much terror and bone-vapour and jeering song in Franz's head that he didn't know what to do. He didn't even know whether these were English children, or ice people, or spider-sleeved men. He only knew they were hunting him and he had to survive.

He lashed out wildly.

'*Ouch! Ouch! You dirty Kraut!*'

One of the figures had ducked away, so Franz dived through the gap he'd left.

'*Get him!*'

But now someone caught hold of his leg, and the ground was suddenly rushing up to meet him. He put out his hands to save himself and landed painfully on his elbows, and before he could get up something heavy had thumped down on his back.

'*Hold him!*'

Franz was pinned down like a speared stag. But he had to survive.

He summoned all his strength. He rolled himself sideways, and the thing on top of him rolled with him.

'*Don't let him go, Hughie!*'

The weight was off his back, but now there were squeezing fingers round his throat. Franz jabbed back hard with an elbow and connected with something, but the cold fingers only clutched more strongly still and above his head the clouds grew nearer, darker, angrier. Franz, desperate, jerked his head back viciously. There was a crack as his skull hit something, and with a howl the fingers at his throat let go.

Franz had to survive.

Franz pushed himself onto his hands and knees. There was a figure in front of him, teeth shining.

Survive.

Franz dived at its shins and the figure went over him and out of sight. There were two yells as it landed, so it might have fallen on one of the others. There was no time to look.

Franz staggered to his feet and ran.

We will hunt here in this chase . . .

But not him. Not this time. He'd survived this time. He left his enemies by the river cursing him.

13

The frost came in the night and stole over the common, stiffening the grey grass and settling a layer of lace over the muddy ground.

Edrin crawled out of her nest. She stood for a moment, holding up her white arms to the stars, admiring the glittering of her gown. It was sleek against her living thighs, and sewn with a waterfall of shining sequins that flashed with the colours of the fighting stars above her.

It was a fine clear night, but cold. The cold didn't matter—only demons disliked the cold—though tonight, oddly, the frost seemed to be biting almost as sharply at her skin as her hunger gnawed at her belly.

She bared her fangs in a snarl and pulled the demon's coat round her thin shoulders. It was almost as if the demon calf, which was so often in her thoughts, was tainting her mind. Making her feel as a demon did. Pulling her away from the stars.

She spat away the image of the demon in a long line of glistening saliva, and made her way silently through the tiger-ripples of the wood. The warmth of the demon's coat did nothing to quell her hunger.

A skittering in the leaves by her feet sent her searching through them urgently, but she found nothing edible but a few woodlice. Linna's snares were empty again, and useless. Edrin cursed. She almost tore them to pieces in frustration.

Edrin stood, still as stone, to listen. Nothing and nothing and nothing. Why were the snares empty? Could she have tied the knots wrong? Well, she was hungry enough now to risk almost anything. She would go to Sia's territory and look at Sia's snares. Not to touch them, of course, still less to take anything. Only to look at the knots. Even if Edrin found a fat rabbit panting out its juicy life, she would leave it where it was.

She would. She would. However much her hunger tormented her.

Edrin got up and walked very softly through the darkness. Sia would be guarding her territory, of course, and lately Sia had had murder in her eyes. But Edrin had to know about the knots.

And there, there Sia was, behind a slender birch. She was watching something, her long body shining silver and ivory through the darkness of the trees.

And yes. There, further on, something else was shining, too.

Larn. It was Larn, bare-chested and strong, his fair hair gleaming. He was standing high up on the huge limb of an oak tree.

Edrin followed Larn's gaze and took in a sharp breath of wonder. Beyond him the saplings in the wide glade were moving—dipping and curtseying as if they were alive.

But they were. Yes, of course they were. Those weren't saplings at all, but a group of stags. They were browsing on the bramble leaves, heads tipped well back to balance their antlers.

Not magic, then. No magic. But—

Larn raised a shining arm. Paused. Edrin saw what was coming and held her breath.

And then—

—Edrin's heart leapt as Larn's spear sped through the darkness and the stags leapt too, clumsily, eyes flashing white with fear. They turned and ran, but one of them soon staggered and went down. It heaved itself up and ran a few ungainly paces, but then it collapsed again.

And lay, panting, stuck with a quivering spear.

All around the common, heads turned as the scent of the stag's blood pumped out into the air. Creatures sniffed and turned to follow the blood trail. Clawed insect feet, soft maggoty feet, hard tacking claws.

Long ivory feet that left shallow almost-demon tracks.

Drawn by the pumping lurching gush of the stag's staggering heart.

Edrin squatted behind a tree and waited her turn. The killer went first, of course. Then after Larn came Sia, the next in strength. She carved herself a fine bloody haunch still hot with death. Then others of the Tribe came, knives ready.

At last Edrin slipped quietly along a shadow and slid her own knife through the stag's congealing flesh. She took her meat up into a tree and ate, rapturously, until her stomach was bloated and her arms and face stank of the sticky blood.

And then at last, squatting on a narrow branch, she licked herself clean.

By the time she had finished even the Tribe-infant, who had had to crawl here, had eaten his fill and was curled, asleep and still bloody, between the whorls of the new-thrusting bracken shoots.

There were small darting shadows round the stag's corpse, now: shadows that rippled like weeds in water. Weasels, probably. Their tiny teeth cut through the flesh with a slight sucking sound.

And now the Tribe began to sing. Their song had demon words, but the music was stolen from the stars.

It was a song of blood. Of hunting.

> *Through liver and through lungs both*
> *The sharp arrow is gone*

Always after a feast came song. After eating the flesh that pulled the Tribe down towards the earth came the music that lifted them towards the stars.

> *That never after in his life*
> *He spoke more words than one*

Edrin opened her mouth and let the melody flow

through her and out of her.

Fight ye, my merry men—she began.

But at once there was a scuttering and scampering and then the swift snapping shut of silence.

Edrin clapped her hands to her mouth in horror. Instead of her voice joining the others' in the silver ribbon of song, it had lurched out of her mouth, wavering, heavy as an owl's.

Like a *demon's*, almost.

Terror overtook her. This constant hunger, and now this terrible change to her voice, must surely be caused by more than her age.

Sia, long and slim and shining, rose up through the darkness. Her cold eyes searched the night, but Edrin had already leapt from her branch and was running, running out of sight before Sia could take a single step.

The wood was silent again for a hundred heartbeats.

'Larn,' said Sia, at last.

Larn made no reply, though the whole wood was listening.

Sia turned her elegant head even further away from him. The starlight made her face into a thing of finely-sculpted planes and hollows. Like a mask, apart from the burning amber eyes.

'The maid Edrin grows weak,' she went on.

Larn's white fingers tightened on the smooth shaft of his spear.

'She caused Linna to be mortally injured,' he pointed out.

Sia ran a hand through her long hair, and her multitude of silver chains chimed with unearthly music, like an echo of an echo of the singing of the stars.

'Only by luck.'

The wood became still again, so that any demon might have walked through the Tribe with no more knowledge of them than a shiver of cold.

Larn put back his head so that the stars shone reflected in his eyes.

'She has been watching the demon calf,' he said. 'And the calf begins to know her, too.'

Sia's lips twitched into a chilly smile. She had watched demons herself. And not just watched them, either. She had sung to them until their minds melted with rapture and they could tell no tales of Tribes or elves or fairy queens.

But Edrin was young. She had not the strength to melt a demon's mind. Edrin might not win a fight with a demon, and that would be perilous for the Tribe. Yes, Larn was right. The demon calf was beginning to know about the Tribe. Know too much.

Larn, languidly, began to sing. It was an old demon song, but this one was not about hunting. This song was about a Tribe enchantment.

> *The queen of fairies took me*
> *To yon green hill to dwell*
> *And pleasant is the fairy land*
> *But an eerie tale to tell.*

Sia's eyes burned into the shadows between the trees.

59

The demon calf needed to be dealt with. Well, Sia had dealt with demons before. She could sing to this calf and melt its little mind. *The queen of fairies took me.* Yes. That could be done.

But that still left Edrin. Edrin, who was growing up.

'Edrin's interest in the calf is very great,' Sia said. 'Disgusting. Not normal. This fascination is drawing her away from the stars. She is close to becoming *not Tribe*, and that is dangerous. We would be safer without her.'

Larn licked one last stain of black blood from the inside of his arm.

'Perhaps,' he said. 'But she is growing. It is a foolish, dizzy time. She may grow back to the Tribe if the demon is no longer here. And I should like to see Edrin grown.'

Sia turned furious, murderous, glowing eyes on him. But Larn sat musing, his hand caressing the shaft of his silver spear.

14

Edrin stood very still, her eyes tight shut to prevent their green gleam betraying her. The thorns of a may tree had caught the demon's coat as she'd fled, and she'd not dared to pull herself free. There were many sharp eyes close by, and she couldn't risk betraying the fact that she was trapped.

So she'd heard the speech between Larn and Sia, and seen the deadly glow of Sia's amber gaze.

Above Edrin's head the stars fired flares across the universe. They had been fighting for millennia—longer even than the uncounted tides of time since the Tribe had stepped out of the moonlit streaks between the trees and begun their own battles.

Edrin heard a twig snap and held her breath. There, across the wood, came the faint sound of footsteps. The feast was over, and Larn and Sia and the Tribe were moving on their separate ways.

Edrin ripped the demon coat angrily out of the clutch of the grey may tree.

She had little hope, now that her voice had betrayed her. The Tribe had discovered that she was changing, and suddenly she was *not Tribe*. An outsider.

She spat. Well, what was the Tribe, anyway? A gathering of skinny paupers, rich only in beauty and song. Why should they preen themselves? They had not a fraction of the skill or strength of demons.

Truth, that was.

Edrin thought about the demon calf (so often she found herself thinking of that stupid ugly demon calf). She kept remembering its fascinating heaviness. Its anger. Its gentleness. Its solitude.

She shivered, and shook all thought of it out of her mind. Sia was going to enchant the demon calf, anyway. Destroy it. Destroy its mind, at least.

Which didn't matter to Edrin. Of course not.

Especially not when Sia was plainly out to destroy Edrin, too.

15

Franz left the house as early as he could the next morning. He grabbed his packed lunch, shouted a goodbye, and slipped out while the Squirrel was in the yard.

Sometimes it was hard to be alone so much. But he was just going to have to get used to it.

He swung his satchel over his shoulder and set out for the common. He had to get his coat back. He really had to. The Wolf and the Squirrel were members of the Nazi party. That meant they didn't believe in protecting anyone weak, anyone stupid, anyone who needed help to survive. Franz could never let them know he couldn't even manage to stop someone stealing his coat.

So he was going back to the common. As for that skeleton . . . well, it hadn't been human, that was sure, so of course it must have been of some sort of animal. And, well, so what? There were animal skeletons all over the common.

As for the melting of the bones, and the voices in his head . . .

He squashed down the fear that was rising again inside him. Whatever it had been, none of it had hurt him. Scared him witless, yes, but not actually hurt him.

And as for the ice maiden (for he still had no other name for her) . . .

Franz thought back. He'd never really seen her properly, but she'd seemed light and thin. Hardly more than a sparkling shadow.

Well, there was no point in being afraid of a shadow, even a coat and egg stealing one. Whatever she was, he wasn't going to be fooled by her again.

Franz had thought it all out. She was hungry and cold. Well, Franz had brought bread and cake to bargain with. He would have brought a jumper, too, but he had so few clothes in England that it would be missed at once.

Franz walked quietly past the squashed-together brick houses of the English town, over the cracked paving stones, along the damp roads.

His squirrelish mother still fussed round Franz, making sure he was fed and warm, but of course she wouldn't carry on like that for long. Oh no, all that fussing was just part of Nature's system. Every sort of animal had to arrange for its young to survive, but once they'd done that they chased their young away. *Fought* them away, even, if they had to. It was Nature. Even the brightest, happiest family would be vicious, then.

Here were the twitching curtains of the Fox and Hounds, and here was the bridge. At least John Coker and his cronies were at school in the mornings.

Franz had been a fool to fight them yesterday. He wasn't sure exactly how it had all started, but his knuckles were bruised so he must have hit someone hard. He shrugged. John Coker and the others had always been going to get him some time. It was just that now the next attack would come sooner. And harder.

Franz crossed the bridge. Ahead of him there was a man striding along who looked a bit like the Wolf, but it couldn't really be him because he was going into the big house by the river, and the Wolf knew no one in the town.

Franz half-wondered yet again where the Wolf went every day. But he only half-wondered; he knew more than he wished to know about the Wolf already.

Franz walked past the house and up towards the common.

There were new lambs in the fields by the road, all tremble-legged and frisk-tailed, their mothers keeping up a chorus of anxious bleating. Franz stopped to watch them. Why were the mother sheep so afraid? There were no lions here any more, no eagles.

The lambs were playing happily, not afraid at all. So was there some instinct which took over their brains as they got older? *Stay with the flock. Keep watch. Run together.*

Well, why not? Franz's mind was changing as he grew up, as he'd begun to understand how things worked. All creatures had to learn the same lessons. *Kill. Run. Fight for your hunting grounds.*

You couldn't blame them.

'It's nothing,' the Wolf had said, steering Franz across the road from the shouting Berlin crowd. 'Just some Gypsies.'

Could you blame the Wolf for letting the Gypsies be taken away? Everything had to defend its territory. Perhaps

Franz's brain would grow and change until it was natural for him to behave like that himself. Until it seemed natural to get rid of anyone who was different. Natural to trust no one.

He left the sheep and made his way up the road towards the common.

16

Edrin's nest was well-hidden inside a tangle of briars. She'd lined it over the centuries with wisps of fence-snagged wool.

She waited until the sun was high, listened carefully, and then crawled out of her nest. The Tribe were mainly creatures of the night, when the moonlight through the trees sliced them into fragments and confusion. The sunrise sent the Tribe into hiding, just as it sent a thousand thousand mice and voles scurrying away from the piercing eye of the kestrel and the snake. Only the hungriest of the Tribe hunted in the daytime.

Edrin should be safe from Sia for the moment.

Edrin squatted down on the drenched grass and searched herself for hairy fleas and blood-swollen ticks. Nests always harboured vermin, but at least that meant she never left her nest unfed.

She yawned widely. Down in the valley the scattering of smoke-pipes that pierced the mist was all she could see of the demon city.

How on earth had demons, *demons*, managed to build something as complicated as that great maze of clay box-houses?

(Demons. In her mind again. Though only, of course, because she was looking at their city.)

Demons were so cunning and strong. Why, it was said that demons could even touch the alder trees that lined the river—and just walking into the shadow of an alder tree was enough to send one of the Tribe half mad with agony. Demons were so strong that Edrin found herself almost envying them, but she brushed all such mad thoughts away. Demons might be strong, but they were not free. They were tied with slave-vines to every other demon they had ever known. How could anyone live, imprisoned like that? How could the demon calf walk, how could it breathe, when it was tied and bound to so many others?

Oh, Sia was wrong, wrong, if she thought Edrin would ever get close to the demon calf. Edrin was alone, and would always be alone. Why, the demon calf was revolting. It was heavy and hot, and she hated the way it prowled through the trees; hated the sudden lift of its head when it sensed something; the cast of its face when it peered after her; its rage; its curiosity; its gentleness.

Its . . .

Edrin blinked her gleaming eyes.

Its *freedom*.

She froze, amazed, as her view of the demon calf widened and changed. Its *freedom*? But how could a demon be free? Demons were all tied together with slave-vines. Except . . .

Edrin shuddered with a sort of excitement, and under the calf's heavy coat the sequins on her dress sparkled like sunlight on wind-lifted water.

Except for this one. That was why the demon calf had

fascinated her. Because it was free. Because it had no slave vines tying it to any others. It wasn't bound to anyone. It was a demon, but it was *free*.

It wasn't its shiny hair that had intrigued her, or its great powerful hands. It was that this demon was *alone*, as she was. It was free of all the bonds which tied the other demons together.

Yes. The demon vines were invisible, but every movement, every breath, had told her that this demon calf was free.

Rich and powerful and *free*.

And that changed everything.

Suddenly she had some hope. Sia would soon kill Edrin if she stayed amongst the Tribe. But if Edrin could work out the demon calf's secret—work out how it lived in the rich demon city but still kept itself free—then she might have a chance, after all. The demon city was huge. There might be some pit where she could hide somewhere in the great maze of it. There might be meat to scavenge (oh, she was so *hungry*!).

She must find the demon calf. Watch it closely, so closely. Work out how its heavy lungs worked. How its bones moved. How it managed to be unlike any other demon she had ever seen in all her centuries of living.

She got up and made her way swiftly, following its familiar musky scent, towards the sludgy edge of the pool.

The demon calf was staring into the green water. It was purple and goose-bumped, shivering without its thick coat. Edrin's stomach twitched with interest and disgust.

She had been careful not to make a sound, but the demon calf looked up as if it had sensed something. Edrin, peering out from behind the trunk of a young beech tree, was sure it hadn't spotted her. But something had alerted it to her presence.

The demon rubbed its stubby arms uneasily.

'I know you're there,' it said.

Its voice was hoarse, and its words juddered roughly through its thick lips. It was looking round in every direction except the right one.

'You took my coat,' it went on, all horribly mauve with tepid blood. 'And I need it back. Or I'll get into trouble, probably.'

Edrin's lips curled with contempt despite her fascination. How was it possible for anything to be so dim-witted? *I'll get into trouble* . . . Why would that matter to her? Why did the stupid creature not say *I'll break your bones!* or *I'll bring a hundred demons here and cut down every tree on the common, and you with them!* Demons had done just that in other places.

Or so the songs said.

The creature picked up a bag from the ground and held it tightly against its tunic as if it was afraid someone might snatch it.

So. It had learned something, then.

And then it said something else in its lurching, blaring voice.

'Are you hungry?' it said. 'Because I'll do a swap with you. My coat for food.'

17

Food.

Edrin's mouth was suddenly filled with juices, and her heart with desire. She had gorged the night before, but she was starving again.

Again. So very soon. She should not need food now for a week. But she did.

She did.

The bag the demon held was big enough to hold half a dozen squirrels. A deer's head. Two brace of fat pheasant. A litter of rabbit kits.

Edrin sniffed, but she could not scent blood. Perhaps the demon lied.

It might be a trap.

But still, her mouth watered.

'I have bread,' said the demon. 'And cake, too. Good English cake.'

Edrin knew nothing of cake, but she had heard of bread. It was a food which demons prized greatly. They even made songs about it. They went to all the trouble of planting the stiff fields of corn to get the seed. And then they burnt it.

Her mouth puckered in disgust—but her eyes remained fixed on the demon's bag.

The demon shifted the bag in its arms. The bag seemed quite heavy, even to the demon's thick limbs. She would be able to gorge herself again with all the food in that bag. She would be able to hide from Sia all through the night and not have to hunt.

She sniffed again. No blood. Definitely no blood.

'I could bring more, too,' offered the demon, its huge eyes darting everywhere but still somehow not able to see her head peering round the tree trunk, even though she was as tall as the demon was and her eyes were as green as emeralds. 'I could bring you more food tomorrow. But I need my coat back first.'

What sort of a fool did it think she was? Why would it bring more food once it'd got what it wanted?

'Eggs,' went on the demon, its eyes searching, searching, but not seeing. 'I could bring you eggs. Big eggs, from hens.'

It squatted there, its stubby body and thick limbs pulsing its heat into the sharp spring air.

Then it opened the bag a little and delved inside.

'Here,' it said, holding out something not quite towards her.

It could sense her cold, she realized suddenly. Just as she could feel its heat, it could feel her cold.

She leaned forward a little, carefully, and sniffed. The thing it held was round and flat and pale, a little like a huge mushroom. What scent it had was not of poison.

As if divining her thought, the demon tore off a piece of the . . . the *stuff*. It was stretchy, spongy, like the tripes of a deer.

The demon put it in its great mouth and chewed.

Edrin leaned forward some more. The sound of the demon's chomping and slavering was unbearable, filling her with deep revulsion but a maddening hunger, too.

The demon's neck was thick. Could she squeeze its throat hard enough to break its spine before it could fight back? She certainly couldn't afford to let it get a grip on her or it would crush her bones to splinters.

But then she didn't *want* to kill it. Not yet. Not while it had secrets she needed to know.

The demon waved the mushroom-thing in her direction. The smell of it came up to Edrin again. It smelt better now she was getting used to it.

Food.

Her hunger rolled massively through her, and her great need dissolved her caution.

She settled her feet carefully. If the demon caught hold of her then it would crush her ribs as easily as she crunched up a mouse.

But . . . but here was *food*.

Edrin stilled her breathing and brought to mind the stars, the twirling, sparkling, fighting stars.

Take me, she whispered.

And at once around her the trees seemed to grow, stretch higher, until they reached the sky. Even the squatting demon grew long and blue-tinged and hardly ugly at all.

Edrin passed a hand in front of her face and saw nothing. Thanks be to the stars. They had received her, and now she was invisible.

She could not stay with the stars for long because every

moment was like hanging onto the edge of a cliff, but as soon as she had the smallest chance ...

... the demon glanced down into its bag again, and at that moment she moved. She leapt across the green shining pool, landed in front of the demon, and snatched.

The demon flinched and ducked away in terror, but its huge hands had tightened instinctively on its bag before she had quite got it away. Oh, and it was so strong, so *strong*! It had only a finger-hold on the bag, but even so its grip was as strong as hers.

No! Greater than hers—for now it had given the bag a tug and suddenly she was falling towards it.

She shrieked with rage and terror. Its whole body jerked as if the sound hurt it, but its great hand had somehow seized her wrist in a hot and crushing grip.

'My coat,' it blared, loud as a thunderstorm. '*I need my coat!*'

Panic and terror and disgust overwhelmed her. She lashed out with her free arm and her legs and head, lunged for its throat with her teeth, shook her white hair into its eyes, screamed shrill foulness.

But its large hot hand still held her, and could have snapped her bones like twigs.

'*I need my coat!*' it kept repeating, doggedly. '*I need my coat!*'

Its deep voice quivered her belly, but she was fighting for her life and its words had stopped having any meaning. She was struggling, kicking, trying to bite—but somehow her face had got something smothering and scratchy wrapped round it, blinding her. So she fought harder, scratching randomly with hands and feet, with the demon's hot breath poisoning the air all round her.

And then somehow she was free, and it was light again, and she'd freed herself from the demon's thick fingers.

But the stars . . . the *stars*! In her fright she'd let herself fall from the realm of the stars!

She leapt away across the pool, pelting over the soft curled leaves until she was far into the woods and there was silence all round her except for the ragged panting of her breath.

Edrin stole back to the pond as soon as the demon had gone. There was a blackbird there, pecking among the windlestraws.

She tried to stalk it, but it cocked its gold-rimmed eye and flew long before she was in pouncing distance.

She spat a curse after it and went over to look at what it had been eating. Yes, she'd thought so: the demon calf was so utterly stupid—so *utterly stupid*—that it had left its food behind, even though it had fought her off. Even though it had somehow managed to snatch its coat back from her during the process, as well.

The squashy mushroom-thing it had left was clammy and tasteless, but it went some way towards filling her belly. And the hunk of stuff beside it—a glistening slab dotted with things like rat droppings—was sweet as sun-warmed berries.

She ate it all hungrily. There was enough nourishment there to keep her alive through the night. She would not need to hunt. She could stay in her nest and not go out into the night-time of the common, where Sia would be waiting for her.

She sat back, licking her fangs. The demon calf was long gone, but the faint trail of its warmth still hung on the air.

It would have gone back to the city, the mysterious demon city. There were tales which said its streets were paved with meat.

The city was where it had got this food. And its clothes, too. And yet somehow it had managed, despite being surrounded by thousands of demons, to keep itself free.

Food, warmth, and freedom, all down in the mysterious demon city.

Edrin wavered. The city was a place of deadly danger. But then so was the common, too. There were dangers everywhere. It was the way of things.

And that trail of warmth was teasing her.

She began to follow it down towards the grey mist which hid the demon city.

18

As soon as Franz was off the common he stopped and did what he could to get his coat clean. Picking off the bits of twig was no problem, but both cuffs had what looked horribly like big bloodstains all over them. Altogether the thing looked as if it'd been dragged through several hedges, a death-scene, and a very wet bog.

Which it might well have been.

His hands were still trembling a bit from those crowded moments by the pool. It had only been the horrible thought that the ice maiden might be trying to kiss him that had shocked him into action. He'd fought back furiously against the screaming fighting invisible ice-cold length of her. Her bones were stick-thin, and he felt sure he could have snapped them like icicles if only he could have got a proper grip on her—but she could move like lightning. It'd only been luck that had got him his coat back.

He rubbed the back of his hand thoughtfully. It was scored with three long scratches, and under his thick woollen socks his shins were throbbing. There'd be bruises there tomorrow.

And after all that he still hadn't seen the ice maiden

properly. He'd definitely seen *something*, as she'd slipped down out of his coat and ducked away from him, but she'd been moving so fast that he still couldn't be exactly sure what he'd seen.

He tried to work it out as he walked down towards the bridge. There'd been sheep-white straggles of hair, and emerald eyes, and a blue tongue . . .

. . . yes, he was almost sure she'd had a blue tongue . . .

. . . and glints of silver. A shiny bracelet of some kind. Thin hands white as bone.

And a desperate fierceness. Yes, that most of all. A *desperate* fierceness.

Wild green eyes and burning-cold fingers that had clawed his tender throat.

Franz was almost at the river, now. He must be careful because John Coker and his cronies would be around here somewhere. They might not have claws, but people were just as vicious as the ice maiden. You could read it in the twitching curtains, and the stony sideways looks; in the gangs of spiteful stone-throwing boys and the—

—*dakka-dakka-dakka-dak!*

Franz jumped. Machine guns!

Dakka-dakka-dakka-dakka!

Machine guns? But this was England. So—

—and so of course it couldn't be machine guns. Of course not. It was danger, though, all the same. There. There, under the bridge. A figure, hiding. It was holding a heavy stick.

Dakka-dakka-dakka-dakka!

The stick jerked viciously as John Coker spat the sound across the meadow.

Franz stepped quickly behind the purplish twigs of a blackthorn bush. John Coker hadn't got a real machine gun, but he'd got a real stick. So where were the other boys?

Dakka-dakka-dakka-dakka!

There. Behind the trunk of that alder tree. Hughie Badrick.

'*Hands hotch!*'

And that was Dick Wright's voice. Yes, there he was, as podgy and straw-haired as ever, over by the scrubby hedge. But *hands hotch*? What on earth did that mean?

And then Hughie raised his hands in surrender, and Franz realized. Dick was trying to speak German. *Hände hoch!* Hands up!

In Berlin there'd been a man who used to stand on the corner of the road. He sold matches. His head was too big, and he couldn't talk, but he was always smiling. If anyone bought some matches he used to do a little jig of joy. His name was Hans.

But then one day Franz was walking along the road with the Wolf when a troop of soldiers had come along checking people's papers. And Hans must have done something wrong because one of the soldiers had shouted *Hände hoch!* and somehow all the matches had gone everywhere.

And then the Wolf had said, rather quickly, that he must have left his wallet at home. So they'd hurried back to the house even though Franz was very worried because Hans couldn't talk, so he couldn't explain things to the soldiers.

Just as they were going inside, someone had shouted something very loudly. And then there had been a slap, so loud it had echoed off the house opposite. And then

79

there'd been a horrible grunting yell.

And Franz had never seen Hans after that.

Franz watched John and Hughie and Dick playing soldiers. It seemed a long time since Franz had played at anything. The boys machine-gunned each other and died horribly again and again.

In the breaks while they recovered from their deadness their voices came up to him over the wet grass.

'If there's a war, right—'

'—my dad says there's bound to be a war.'

'—all right, then. But if there's a war, I'm going to be a machine-gunner. *Dakka-dakka-dakka-dakka-dak!*'

'Death to the Nazis!'

'Down with Hitler!'

'Death to all spies! *Dakka-dakka-dakka-dakka!*'

'They shoot spies with rifles, not machine guns, you clot!'

Pause.

Then:

'Do you think we ought to tell someone about the Kraut's dad?'

That was Hughie who said that, he of the blotchy cheeks and tiny round spectacles.

'He's vicious, that Kraut,' said Dick, bitterly. 'Just look at my eye!'

'There's nothing wrong with your eye.'

'That's only because I'm a fast healer.'

'But the Kraut's dad . . .'

Another pause.

'He must be planning something pretty complicated,'

John Coker said. 'This is the third time he's come back to England.'

'Yes, but we've still got no idea what it is,' said Dick. 'No one's going to listen to us, are they, if we don't know what it is.'

'We'll just have to keep on watching him, then, that's all,' said John. 'See if we can catch him in the act. And *then* we'll get him.'

'String him up!'

'Shoot him down!'

'*Dakka-dakka-dak! Dakka-dakka-dak!*'

When it began to get dark the boys stashed their machine gun sticks inside a bush and went home to their suppers.

Franz watched them go, their voices still echoing in his mind.

Death to the Nazis.

Death to all spies.

Catch him in the act.

What *were* the Squirrel and the Wolf doing here in England, month after month? Far away from Berlin, where they had important friends and were rich and powerful?

If there was a war . . .

If there was a war, Hughie and John and Dick would do the same as everyone else. Just like the deer or the sheep or the ants did. Or the people of Berlin. Because they were animals who were threatened. Fight for their territory. Hunt to survive.

Franz went quietly home.

The net curtains of the Fox and Hounds twitched as he went past.

19

The demon calf had been hiding from those other demons for so long that Edrin had nearly fallen asleep on the oak branch where she lay watching them. But now at last it was moving, trudging along the harsh grey road towards the demon bridge.

Edrin followed it. She kept the hedge between them, but still she caught its scent once or twice—the hot, disturbing smell of it. It sent a thrill of fear and excitement fizzing through her veins.

She carefully skirted the meadow, keeping well away from the alder trees planted along the river bank. Demons knew little about the Tribe, but they knew enough to plant mind-stabbing alders to protect their city.

Edrin caught the scent of something else just as she reached the last tree before the bridge.

It was the scent of death, oozing out at her from the city of the demons. No, worse than death, it was the scent of never-living. Of stone laid over fertile ground; of baked clay roofs that blocked out the stars.

She halted, shivering. That was more horrible than anything she'd ever imagined, to live amongst death. Perhaps cutting themselves off from everything that breathed, grew, flourished, was the secret of the demons' strength.

The bridge in front of her was blue-tinged in the darkening air. It was deserted, but across it lay herds of demons, thousands of them, all tied together in a sticky web of slavery.

No, not quite all of them. Not quite all.

Edrin's heart began to tick fast inside her. Sia could walk invisibly and safely through this place, but Edrin's own hold on the stars was weak. She might not be able to stop herself from falling into visibility. She might fall into sight when she was surrounded by great-limbed wet-eyed demons.

But the demon calf was across the bridge, now. She must follow it now if she was going to, or she would lose it.

Suddenly, she didn't want to lose it.

She slid out from behind the last tree before the bridge.

Franz knocked on the door of his house with relief. There'd been a draught of freezing air following him ever since he'd crossed the bridge. His skin had been quivering with the dread of ice-cold fingers clutching at him from behind every lamp post and wall.

The Squirrel opened the door. She looked anxiously up and down the street, and then she smiled at Franz.

'Come in, come in, my darling,' she said. 'You must be cold. Come in.'

Franz looked away from her smile. It looked friendly, but it was just a trick. He knew that. It wasn't easy to resist, for all that. It would have been the simplest thing in the world to smile back, to let himself be sucked into the pretence that everything was all right. That she was warm, devoted, kind, loving.

He gritted his teeth and remembered Berlin. How the Squirrel had smiled and rearranged her furs as she tripped past things that should have filled her with horror; things that should have haunted her nights beyond hope of rest.

That worked. At once the Squirrel's smile became nothing more than a painted curl, and the Squirrel herself no more than Franz's landlady and cook.

But he was glad to leave that icy trail of air behind and follow her into the damp shelter of the house, all the same.

Edrin, a little way up the demon road, pressed herself into a wall made of mutilated bushes. She was close to puking with sheer horror. The adult female demon who'd come to the door had given the calf no time to defend itself. It'd attacked the calf at once. Vines like ropes had shot out of the female's eyes and deep, deep into the calf's flesh, pulling it into the house.

Edrin hadn't seen them, exactly, but she'd sensed them strongly. Was that because she'd been watching the demon calf for so long that she could sense when he was attacked?

The calf had fought off the female—withered the female's vines to dust before the door had shut behind it—but the strong sense Edrin had had of those things burrowing like snakes through the demon's flesh . . .

The only reason Edrin was not sick was because she was so empty. *Hungry.* Again. Again. Filled with yearning for ...

... but what could it be for, but food?

Edrin gulped in deep breath after deep breath: did her best to calm her frantic ticking heart. Those vines were terrible things, evil and devilish, but the demon calf had fought them off. (*Thank all the stars*, she nearly thought— but that would have been ridiculous. As if she cared.)

Edrin's first instinct was to go away, right away from this dreadful place, back to the common; but those vines had shaken her courage and she couldn't face travelling back along the stony demon streets.

She needed somewhere to hide. Well, that clay wall over there joined the back of the demon calf's house. If she climbed over it she would be able to hide in the shadows of the star-leaved ivy that hung all over it. Then she could watch the box-house of the demon calf. Watch the lamplight shining on his hair through the bottle-stuff openings in the walls. (On *its* shining hair, she meant, of course: on *its* shining hair.)

It was strange, mad, ridiculous, but sometimes she almost forgot her hunger when she was watching the demon calf.

She looked both ways to be sure she was alone, and then she pulled herself easily over the wall, for she was strong.

Franz washed his hands at the kitchen sink. The water was so cold that the green soap sat in his hands like a stone and refused to lather.

This English house had no garden, only a concrete yard enclosed by an ivy-covered wall. He'd seen robins there, lately, and had been hoping they might nest.

The ivy looked bulkier than usual that evening, more shadowy.

He hoped it was a sign of spring.

20

Edrin stood amongst the ivy leaves, watching. Sometimes she caught glimpses of the demon calf: its straight brows, its smooth hair, its warmth-tinged skin. A third demon had arrived in the box-house now, a full-grown male.

Why in the name of all the stars did demons live like that, in the same box, together?

But she knew why: the female and male were tied with slave-vines. They would have no choice but to live together. It was said that demons who were kept apart from each other felt such pains that they could take no pleasure in anything. And that was really true, it was said, even though demon females were heavy and ugly and hot, hot, hot. Yes, it was certainly true. There were even more demon songs about vines than there were about hunting.

This demon calf was different, though. It was bound by no slave-vines. It was free.

So why did it live with those others?

Well, the food would be enough of a reason. And this box-house was full of all sorts of other precious things, too. She could see that this demon place was stuffed with seats, and tables, and the stars only knew what else: so many things that they could not even walk straight from one part of the box to another.

The female's shoes were good. The female had come out into the yard to visit the turd shelter and Edrin had seen them (demons ate and drank so much they . . . but that didn't bear thinking about). Heeled, the demon's shoes were, and shiny, and a matching pair. Edrin *wanted* them.

Before long, through the stench of the turd shelter, food smells began stealing from the box-house. It was enough to drive her mad with longing.

Franz bit into the piece of cake his mother passed to him. It was delicious.

'Well?' asked the Squirrel, watching him anxiously. 'Is it good?'

'Very good,' said Franz, politely.

The Squirrel smiled her brittle English smile.

'I think now I have understood the oven,' she said. 'And I think also that I begin to tolerate English food.'

The Wolf raised an eyebrow.

'Any chance that you might even get to *like* it one day?' he asked.

The Squirrel hesitated.

'Perhaps. But many things I shall always miss. Pickled fish. *Götterspeise.*'

Franz looked sharply from one to the other of them.

'Always?' he echoed. 'Aren't we *ever* going home to Berlin, then?'

But the reply was so long coming Franz didn't bother to listen to it. It plainly wasn't going to be true.

Death to all spies.

What *did* the Wolf do during all the long days he spent in England?

Franz shrugged.

Edrin watched the squares of yellow light disappear from the bottle-stuff openings of the demons' box. That meant the demons had gone to their rest (in *beds*, the songs said, whatever they were).

She squinted upwards, past the smudges of the scudding clouds to the darker regions of the sky. The street lamps were fizzing out a hard star-quenching light, but she could just make out a great gobbet of sapphire fire tearing through the darkness. And . . . and, yes, there was the mighty ruby flare of the reply.

This city was a desolate place, but even here the stars were still above her. Still fighting. And would be for ever, whether she were there to see them or not.

Well, like the glorious stars she must keep on fighting. Fighting and hunting and trying to survive.

Edrin took a deep breath—and scented something. Yes, now she was not distracted by the demon calf, her senses were sharper. And . . . yes. Through all the demon and death smells of the city, she could detect the scent of *blood*.

Edrin climbed swiftly over the wall and slipped along between the lines of clay box-houses. The demons were at their rest, so she went unseen except for a single slinking cat. The cat was fat, but sadly nimble: it slipped ghost-like out of her reach, jumped elegantly onto the top of a wall, and vanished.

Edrin cursed quietly and turned a corner. The demon box-houses here had huge bottle-stuff openings in them.

Windows, they were. She remembered that now. They were called *windows*.

Edrin pressed her nose against the silky surface and peered in.

Clothes. This box was full of clothes, racks of them. Fine silks and soft wool. She could break this bottle-stuff quite easily and then . . .

. . . and then make enough noise to bring a whole herd of demons down upon her.

She turned away in spitting frustration and went on.

And here it was. Here at last was the place where her nose had been leading her. A faintly gleaming silver barrel more than half as high as she was.

Scented with *food*.

The top of the barrel was heavy. It chimed deeply as she lifted it off. She put the thing down very cautiously on the square stone paving slabs and looked inside.

It was full of wood-sheet parcels. Oh, and yes, rising to meet her was the rich metallic scent of *blood*.

She tore open the first of the parcels. Here were bones. They weren't quite clean, either, though they'd been fire-tainted in the stupid demon way.

Under the bones were scrapings from some sort of root. The idiot demons had stored the valuable skin here, in a barrel in the street, where anyone might steal it.

She sucked greedily at the bones, devoured the root-skin, and then ripped open another parcel and found a big delicious bird carcass. She ripped open more parcels and more, greedily, until she got to the bottom of the barrel. The meat there was foul with decay, so she moved on, leaving the silver lid gleaming faintly on the stone paving and the path strewn with scraps.

She found another barrel quite soon, but there was less in that one worth eating.

The next, though, was alive with juicy wriggling maggots.

Edrin had eaten her way along a whole row of demon boxes before she thought to check the stars. The night was well advanced and every demon in the city would be in its deepest sleep.

What now? Her belly was full, but somehow she was still hungry. Yes, she was still *hungry*.

But how could she be? What could she be hungry for, if not for food?

She sniffed the air, searching for something she didn't understand. Scents died soon in this horrible place, but . . .

The blustery wind had swept the sky clear, and now in the light of the shiny moon a whole trail of silvery barrel lids were gleaming up at the stars.

And Edrin found herself, for some reason she did not understand (surely it was nothing to do with the fact that demons were made of *meat*) slipping back along this glimmering trail, back towards the box-house of the demon calf.

To the one who'd that day brought her a gift of food. To the one she'd been watching for many months. To the one whose presence made her forget her hunger and her cold. To the demon who walked alone.

21

Franz opened his eyes to the glistening moon.

He lay watching its silver fingers slide through the shadows and onto his bed. In another few minutes it would find him.

Except that it was only the moon. A lump of rock. Of course it couldn't find him.

Although . . .

. . . it was strange, but Franz did feel as though *something* was searching for him.

He sat up and pulled one of his blankets round him. A shaft of moonlight touched his shoulder, silvering the filaments of the wool. He got out of bed and went to the window. Outside the dark slates of the long rows of houses were glimmering slightly. All those houses. All those people. Towns, cities, countries full of them.

What was the moon shining over tonight?

Pictures formed swiftly in Franz's mind, each as sharp as the edge of the moon. He tried to close his mind against them but it was too late, they were inside him and there was no door to shut.

Black marching boots.

Breaking glass. (That was from the last night before they'd come to England. Franz hadn't really been awake most of the time, he knew that, but he certainly remembered running crowds, and breaking glass, and people hammering on the door.)

That picture led on to others.

Frau Rosen on her hands and knees in the street.

The Gypsies.

The deaf girl who'd lived by the park.

Hans who sold matches, who grinned and grinned and couldn't speak at all.

And everywhere, over everything, flags, walls, people, the hunting four-legged spiders.

Franz leaned his forehead against the cold window, trying to forget.

And then down in the concrete English yard there was a noise and Berlin vanished from his mind.

It wasn't a loud noise, but Franz knew exactly what it was.

The kitchen window didn't close properly. The frame had swollen in the endless damp of the English winter and the sash no longer quite shut. The Wolf had wedged folded newspaper in the gap to plug the whistling draught.

And now someone was trying to pull the window open.

Someone was trying to break into the house.

Franz opened his mouth to call the Wolf—but there was someone out in the yard listening and he wasn't sure if that was the best thing to do. Instead he went cautiously out onto the landing and across to the other bedroom door.

The landing was no more than a square metre of freezing lino. At the bottom of the stairs there was a green speckled mirror. It was reflecting the moonlight in an under-water sort of way.

Franz's hand was on the handle of the Wolf's bedroom door when something moved. He turned his head quickly. There was a black shape moving in the green depths of the moonlit mirror. A figure. Someone very very thin . . .

Franz carefully stepped down a couple of stairs. He kept to the side of the treads so they didn't creak.

He could see much better, then.

The figure in the mirror was tugging fiercely at the paper wedged in the window.

It wasn't human.

Franz went down three more careful steps. He could see straight into the kitchen, then.

Then quite suddenly the thing outside pressed its face against the window and Franz found himself staring at a white flattened nose and two hungry eyes. He saw everything, all in a flash: the straggles of hair, the skeletal thinness. Franz, his mind still clouded with thoughts of Berlin, was suddenly pierced with the memory of the Gypsy girl he'd seen marched along the street.

He ran down the last few stairs and into the kitchen. For a moment the thing at the window froze, staring.

And then it turned and ran.

'Wait,' Franz whispered urgently, fumbling at the bolt on the back door. 'It's all right. I'm your friend! I'll help. Do you understand? Wait!'

Franz managed to draw back the bolt and turn the awkward black key. He stepped out into the freezing air.

'I'll be your friend!' he said, as loudly as he dared.

Nothing. Not even a stirring of a leaf.

Where could she be? Invisible again?

Franz hesitated. Then he went to the bread bin, laboriously cut off a thick slice of bread, and put it on the doorstep.

'There,' he whispered, into the night. 'Have it. Have it. It is for you.'

He was back in bed before he made up his mind.

What he'd just seen hadn't been an ice maiden. Not an ice maiden like the one in the story, anyway. Now he had seen her properly he knew she wasn't. She was fierce and young and alone and lost: but she was not an ice maiden. She wasn't seeking to clutch him to her in a kiss of death, or to lure him away anywhere. How could she be, when she was lost herself?

So what was she?

Someone poor and hungry.

Someone not even human.

Someone backward, a dead-end, not evolved properly. A stranger. Someone foreign. Someone *other*.

Franz thought again of Berlin. Of the four-legged hunting spiders of his dreams. Of Gypsies, and Frau Rosen. Of the Squirrel and the Wolf dressing in their finest clothes and laughing at parties with powerful clever men. Of Nazis. Of poor Hans the match seller. Of crossing the road because things were complicated. Of strong people, and weak people, and the need of every creature on earth to fight and hunt and kill to survive.

It would make no sense to have anything to do with the ice maiden (or whatever, *who*ever she was: the name would have to do for now, for it was all he had). No sense at all. She was still dangerous, that was for sure.

It made no sense to waste energy pitying her, either. The weak must fail. It was simple, and inescapable, and true. That was what you learned as you grew up. It was what the creatures of the common had shown him again and again, the fox and the kestrel and the stag.

Fight for your life. Maintain your hunting territory. Kill outsiders.

That was what it meant to be an adult. That was what the Nazis stood for. Strength and cleverness and maintaining territory. It all made sense.

But still, he pitied her. And he was going to help her if he could.

And suddenly for the first time for months he found himself lifted by a sort of hope. It might make no sense to help her. It might be nonsense as far as the Nazi scientists were concerned. But then the Nazis knew nothing about the ice maiden.

The night was cold, but Franz's heart was suddenly pumping hot fast blood through his body.

The Nazis knew nothing about the ice maiden. That was true, really true. They knew nothing at all about her. And if their scientists didn't know about the ice maiden then they didn't know very much at all. So . . .

Franz gasped with sudden realization.

. . . so that meant the Nazis might be wrong about other things, too. They thought they knew everything, but they didn't. And so all their ideas about weak people having to be destroyed might be wrong, too.

Perhaps *all* the Nazis' ideas were wrong.

Franz sat in his chilly bed, shivering with cold and excitement.

If the Nazis were wrong, then that changed everything. Everything.

It meant—he swallowed convulsively—perhaps it might even mean he didn't have to be a killer or a hunter. Perhaps it meant he didn't even have to be alone.

Perhaps it wouldn't be so stupid to make friends with the ice maiden.

Franz was too agitated to sleep. He kept getting up to check the empty yard. In the end he got out of bed into the moon-striped darkness for one last time. He wedged his chair firmly under the handle of the door, and then he felt carefully all round the room, even under the bed.

When he was sure there was no one else there he went back to bed, this time to sleep.

With a kiss-preventing scarf tied tightly round his mouth.

Just in case.

The food the demon had put out for Edrin was poor stuff, damp and bloodless. What scent it had was mostly of the demon's hand.

She held it to her nose, and sniffed deeply. Demon musk. But . . .

. . . she sniffed at the food again. And again, for the scent was making something she didn't understand stir inside her. It was a kind of excitement. Or perhaps it was hunger, after all. The demon had great wads of flesh on its body. Great haunches of meat.

She shuddered a little, perplexed. She'd eaten frog and snake and maggot and crow, but eating demon . . .

Surely she could not want to eat a *demon*?

She looked up at the faint stars.

What was she becoming?

The sky was beginning to pale. The sun would rise soon, and the city's streets would be filled with plodding fleshy demons.

The very thought of being surrounded by all those heavy, musky bodies made her feel sick with revulsion, thank all the stars.

No, she did not want to eat a demon.

So what *did* she want?

The common. Suddenly she wanted the common. She wanted to hear the sap surging in the trees, and see the buds swelling and setting forth a million million intricately pleated new leaves. She wanted to feel a thousand lives around her every step.

She wanted . . .

. . . she wanted to know more of the demon calf. She'd watched it and watched it, but watching was not enough. She needed to get closer to it. Not to eat it. Not to eat it, but . . .

This demon city was not the best place to watch the demon calf, anyway. She understood that now. In the city the demon stayed in its clay box-house behind its brittle windows and she was always at a distance.

There were better places where she could get close to it.

And the common was calling her.

Edrin made her way silently through the lifeless ugly streets and across the bridge.

Dawn was breaking as she stepped into the grey shade of the woods. She halted, listening to the first chirrups of the birds. Somewhere in this place was Sia, who hated her. Somewhere in this place was Larn, who had been watching her, and would be watching her still. Larn, who was strong and beautiful, and wanted something from her that she did not understand.

Edrin was very tired. She slipped through the spring-soaked bracken and birch and ancient oak to her nest, and something like safety.

22

Franz woke to daylight. He had several threads of wool stuck between his teeth, but his scarf lay in a straggle on the floor where he must have thrown it during the night.

He felt much older, somehow: as if at last he'd understood something he'd been groping towards for a long time.

And he found he was quite sure what he should be doing.

'When are we going home?' Franz asked, at breakfast, interrupting the Squirrel in the middle of a long story about the endless dampness of English laundry.

The Wolf frowned at him, but he replied patiently.

'That's not decided, yet, Franz.'

'Are Mother and I going to stay here for ever?'

There was the usual pause while the Wolf worked out some suitable lie. Then the Squirrel laughed. Her nervous English laugh.

'But it is so interesting here,' she said. 'And it is spring at last. We must see the famous English spring, mustn't we. And you love watching the wild creatures on the common so much. There is no hurry at all to go home.'

Franz found that he'd clenched his fists.

'But *are we going to stay here for ever?*' he asked, yet again.

The Wolf and the Squirrel exchanged quick glances.

'You know perfectly well that our home's in Berlin,' the Wolf said, not quite so patiently. 'The business is, too. This is just a holiday, Franz.'

'But Mother doesn't *like* being here,' Franz persisted. 'Mother's afraid to go out of the house in case people attack her because she's a foreigner!'

He spoke angrily, but all the time there was still some part of him that was saying: *explain, please explain. Make it so I can believe you.* Because that glimpse of the ice maiden's half-starved face had changed many things. People were animals, of course they were. They had to hunt, and sometimes they might have to fight for their territory and even their lives. But at the same time to live in that way was not human at all.

He found that he desperately wanted his parents to be human.

The Wolf was running his finger up and down the newly-shaved skin over his jawbone.

'Well, it's been jolly good for you both to have a change of scene, in any case,' he said, and put his newspaper back up in front of his face.

Oh, it had been a change of scene, all right. A change from Berlin, where the Wolf and the Squirrel were rich and happy and part of everything. Until one day a crowd had thrown stones through a foreigner's window and frightened his family into running away.

As if there were anywhere to run.

The Squirrel had begun feverishly to stack plates and bits of cutlery.

Franz looked across the great distance that separated him from the Squirrel and the Wolf. He'd thought the miles and miles between them had been to do with growing up. With independence, strength, cleverness. He'd thought there'd been no choice about it—that it was the only way to survive.

That everyone had to be in some way a Nazi.

But suddenly all that had changed.

'Are we going back to Berlin?' he demanded, once again.

The Wolf spoke, dangerously evenly, through his newspaper.

'We've discussed this, Franz.'

'No we haven't,' said Franz. 'You've never even answered me, let alone discussed anything. Have you.'

The Squirrel looked up, her face pale and anxious.

'But Father has told you we need to go back because of the house and the business,' she began, 'and—'

'*No!*'

The Squirrel jumped, clutching her hands to her throat, and Franz found he'd hit the table hard.

The Wolf folded up his newspaper and swigged off his tea. He got to his feet.

'There's no need to shout, Franz,' he said.

But there was every need to shout.

'Why will you never give me a proper answer?' Franz demanded.

The Wolf was shrugging himself into his greatcoat.

'I'm afraid I haven't time to talk now,' he said, as he did up the buttons.

'But why not?' asked Franz, in exasperation. '*What's the hurry, if you're on holiday?*'

But the Wolf was already opening the front door and putting on his hat. Franz had time only to say:

'Are you going to the house by the river again?' before the door closed firmly behind the Wolf's long back.

The little room turned dark for a moment as his grey figure went past the window.

'Franz,' said the Squirrel, her face frightened and very pale. 'All this—it is not easy to explain. And you are too young—'

'—*no!*' He really shouted, then. 'Do you really think I don't understand?' he went on, furiously. 'Do you really think I couldn't see what was happening in Berlin? Me, who's always watched animals? Do you think I didn't *notice*? Or realize what the Nazis, your rich powerful friends the Nazis, were doing? What they plan to do? Do you really think I don't know about Frau Rosen, or the Gypsies, or that deaf girl who lived by the park?'

The Squirrel stared at him, white as ice. She opened her mouth, but he swept on before she could speak.

'Do you think I haven't wondered where Father goes all day when he's here?' he demanded. 'Has he even told *you* where he goes, or do you just tell yourself that's a matter for cleverer heads than yours?'

'Franz,' said the Squirrel, 'Franz—'

'—because I'll tell you where he goes,' Franz went on,

too wound up to listen. 'He goes down to a house by the bridge, to spend the day with people he's been pretending he doesn't know. *Why?*'

'Franz,' said the Squirrel, pleadingly. 'Franz, you cannot think—'

But Franz had got up. He didn't want to hear anything she had to say.

But he stopped at the bottom of the stairs.

'I'm not going back,' he said. 'I'm never going back. Not to Berlin. Not to be a Nazi. Never.'

And with that he ran up the stairs to his room.

The Squirrel came upstairs, later, but he'd put his chair under the handle of his door again so she couldn't get in.

He waited until she was out at the washing line, and then he slipped downstairs, helped himself to as much food as he could lay his hands on, and went out.

As he walked through the town he found that what he'd told the Squirrel was true. He was *never* going back to Berlin. Never.

So now he was really alone, he realized, suddenly. Absolutely alone. There was nowhere he belonged. It was ridiculous: he'd finally decided he wanted to be with people, and he had not a friend in the world.

He walked down towards the river past the twitching curtains at the Fox and Hounds. There was a grey man striding along in front of him, and this time Franz recognized the Wolf straight away. As Franz watched, the Wolf turned down the driveway of the house by the bridge.

105

Franz paused at the green-painted gate. The grounds of the house went down to the river, and he could see why John Coker and the others had found the meadow a good place to keep watch. All Franz could see from the gate was a decayed-looking garden and some muddy gravel. There was a tall mast in the garden. It might have been a flagpole, except that the English didn't seem to go in for flags, much.

Flagpoles didn't usually have quite such elaborate lightning-conductors, either.

Radio mast?

Radio *transmitter*?

Franz thought about going a little way along the drive; but as soon as he set foot on the gravel a man with a sentry's look about him stepped out from behind a tree.

Franz turned and hurried away.

23

Edrin squatted in her nest. She should be sleeping, but she was restless, and cold, and hungry again. Was she going to be hungry for ever (not that *for ever* was probably going to be very long), plagued by this hunger that food did not ease? Would she always be shivered by this cold that left her searching for some shelter that was always beyond her reach?

She scratched, found a louse, and cracked its hollow body between her teeth.

'*Where are you?*'

Edrin jumped. That voice was close. But then she cursed, and crouched lower still in her nest. That was the demon calf, of course, bellowing about the common and reminding all the Tribe of her existence.

'*I've come to visit you!*'

The fool. The fool. Did it really imagine she'd come out to meet it? Stand before it, so that it could shoot slave-vines out of its eyes and make her its slave for ever? If she was going anywhere near this demon then *she* was going to be the hunter and *it* was going to be the prey.

'*Hello!*'

She was safe enough in her nest, for it was well-hidden inside its straggle of brambles. A hound might sniff it out, but never a demon. But still she found herself cowering like a mouse in a hawk's shadow as the demon's voice echoed round the common.

'*I've brought you some more food!*'

Could the wretched thing not *hold its tongue*?

'*Hello! Hello!*'

Its bellowing was so loud that every creature from the demon pits to the screaming alders by the river must hear it.

'*I want to help you!*'

Go away, then. Go away. Give up trying to find me. Go back to the city where you belong. Don't you realize you have everything anyone could ever want?

(Then why did it seem so lurking and miserable? Well, because it was a fool, of course, a demon clod.)

'*Where are you?*'

Edrin gritted her teeth. Surely the demon calf must give up this shouting soon. She could only hope the Tribe were sleeping so deeply that all this bellowing was nothing more to them than a shadow of a dark dream.

But she had no sooner thought that than there came a new voice weaving through the thin black branches of the wood. Edrin raised her head sharply.

The voice came from the darkest part of the common behind the pool; a high shrill trail of sound, light and deadly as a spider's web.

A Tribe voice, raised in song.

It floated along the moist breeze, thread-like and

chilling, beyond the range of demon ears.

> *'We will not tell what men we are*
> *Nor whose men that we be.'*

Long ago, in a time of fire and ice and strangling vines, demons had come to the common and attacked the Tribe's hunting grounds. The Tribe had fought them with spear and star and song.

And triumphed.

> *'But we will hunt here in this chase*
> *In spite of thine and thee.'*

Tribe song could not be heard by demons, but a demon could be cast in thrall by it all the same. A Tribe song sung by someone full of spite and power could wipe a demon's brain quite empty.

That was Sia's voice. And Edrin could hear its purpose. She shivered.

24

Franz had walked round most of the common, but he'd seen nothing, not even the trotting backs of the shadowy deer, or the smoke-grey rabbits, or the black cawing crows.

It wasn't until he was making his way towards the place where he'd found the skeleton that he heard . . . well, perhaps he didn't actually *hear* anything. But something ran through his mind all the same. Something delicate and cold, like a trickle of moonlight.

He'd go back to the pool, he decided, suddenly—or *something* decided. That would be the best thing. He'd sit down by the green pool. Rest there, and wait. Perhaps the ice maiden might come to meet him in her silver gown.

He turned and made his way back through the trees. The common was coming to life again after the winter, and there were urgent fingers of growth reaching out all round him as if to grab him. As if to stop him.

The pool was shining green, like the eye of a great beast.

Franz took off his coat, folded it into a cushion, and sat down to wait.

★ ★ ★

Sia's song was too high for the poor fool of a demon to hear, but it went into its ears, all the same. Sia, lounging easily in a beech tree, stroked a shimmering ribbon of her dress and opened her mouth wide.

> *'Oh I will hunt here in this place*
> *In spite of thine and thee.'*

Franz shuddered a little, though not from cold. There was a strange English expression: *someone's walking over my grave*; suddenly that was how Franz felt.

> *'Through liver and through lungs both*
> *My sharp arrow is gone.'*

There was a cruel smile in Sia's lovely voice, if only Franz could have heard it.

> *'Oh fight then, demon, whilst ye may*
> *For thy life-days are gone.'*

Franz massaged his ears irritably. They'd started tingling, itching, as if a tiny bee had flown into them—though he could actually hear no sound at all except for the scornful laughter of a far away woodpecker.

Franz turned his attention back to the pool. A finger of sunlight had found its way through the morning haze. It had turned the skin of a lurking frog almost to gold. That was odd. Franz had never seen a golden frog before.

He rubbed his ears again, but it didn't help because the itchy feeling seemed to have burrowed itself right into his head.

> '*And so tomorrow brings your bier*
> *Of birch and hazel grey*
> *And clouds shall let fall weeping tears*
> *To wash your bones away.*'

Sia's white lips widened in a smile of contempt, of triumph, as she sang. Demons were so easily enthralled, and this thing was only a calf: what little wit it had was soon addled.

She threw back her head and laughed, so that tendrils of frost curled through the air and furred the needle buds of the beech tree. This demon's mind was already turned towards a Tribe-female, and that made it the easiest thing in the world to scramble its idiot brain.

Sia opened her mouth and sang on.

The pool was dazzling, fascinating, as if the sun were trapped beneath the green surface. Against its radiance the curly fronds of the water weed hung darkly, like the long rib-cages of snakes.

The thought of snakes jolted Franz a little. He sat up, blinking. He'd nearly been asleep. It was almost as if the glowing of the pool had hypnotized him. As if the glowing of the water had swum into his mind and . . .

. . . and . . .

. . . and never mind. The greenness was soothing and silky and sleepy, after the ear-tickling of . . .

. . . whatever it had been.

And the swaying of the trees was . . .

. . . as gentle as a cradle and as peaceful as a dream . . .

Franz sighed. It was pleasant, here, away from the warring world. Even the tickling-buzz of the fly, or whatever it was, had settled itself so deep into his mind that he hardly noticed it any more.

He nodded, pleased. He'd found out how to ignore it.

Clever.

And now look, here was something new. A sharper brightness up in that tree. Something sparkling, silver as a sun-flashed fish.

He turned his suddenly heavy head to look at it.

It was a woman.

Demon! Demon!

Here I am.

Here!

Here, *fool!*

Do you want me, then?

Does your heavy heart pump great gouts of blood when you see me?

Do your purblind eyes feast on my beauty?

But, there, don't be feared, little hunter. Don't be feared. Don't you want to catch me and bind me to you with slave-vines? Possess me for ever?

Eat me?
Come, then. Come hither.
Yes, yes.
That's right.
Closer.

25

Edrin's nest was too far away for her to hear much of Sia's song, but still the music shivered her, raised the fine fair hairs on her neck.

It was a hunting song. A fighting song. A song of death.

She wrapped her skinny arms round her head to blot out the sound, but still the cool music eased itself in irresistibly through her pores.

Almost, she could feel the melting of the demon calf's mind.

She gritted her teeth. If Sia was enchanting the calf then there was nothing Edrin could do about it. So what if the demon calf's mind was destroyed?

Oh, but she was hungry, *hungry*, with a force that stabbed her like a hunting spear.

It wasn't even as if Sia were actually killing the demon. Sia *could* make it dead, of course. She could make it drown itself in the pool. But Sia wouldn't do that: demons were so tied to each other with slave-vines that killing one demon would alert untold numbers of others to the danger that lurked on the common.

Of course this demon was only young—a calf—but,

oddly, the death of even one single small calf sent dozens of demons into paroxysms of . . .

. . . Edrin did not know what to call it, but she had seen it for herself. There was a demons' burial ground hard up against the woods, and she had watched the demons' faces when small coffins were lowered into the earth. Faces white and waxen and empty, so that they were almost like Tribe-faces—though ugly, of course, with the demon ugliness that sickened to the guts.

Sia's song wound round the naked trees and through the grey air. All around the common creatures would be cowering away from its terrible purity, and Edrin cowered with them. Only the demon calf would be basking, enthralled, as the song's power stole into its ears and scoured clean its skull.

It would be in bliss: shining-haired, great-limbed, all care and passion stilled. Soon its mind would warp and twist until it was destroyed, melted away, killed, and only its great body would remain.

The other demons would not understand what had happened. Death roused them (some of them, anyway) to anger and revenge: if a demon corpse were found here, the common would soon be crawling with herds of them, tainting the spring air with their scent. But a demon with a melted, helpless, idiot mind only bound those around it together with ever tighter slave-vines.

Edrin did not understand it. The best thing, the sensible thing, was to kill anyone useless. Anyone who would never be any profit, or who was a bother or a danger. But demons . . . well, they were crazy. It was the only explanation.

Demons did mad things all the time. Why, a demon might even have helped Linna out of the pit and mended her bones. Perhaps they might even have fed Linna until she were strong enough to hunt again and catch food that they might have had themselves.

Yes, demons really were sometimes as mad as that.

Oh, but would Sia's song never end? It wailed on and on until Edrin was half mad herself. She clasped her thin hands as tightly to her ears as she could, but she couldn't stop the music sending cold fingers through her bones.

The demon calf's mind would not last long, now. That was good, because then Edrin would be free of it. She did not know why it had ever become interested in her, anyway. All her life she had avoided demons, as she avoided anything else dangerous and revolting, like fox turds or hornets. And avoiding demons had always been the easiest thing in the world, for they crashed about and bellowed like rutting stags.

Not that this demon calf had crashed about, or bellowed very much, either. It had spent most of its time being quiet and still. Watching things. Not even hunting, she realized now, but just watching the creatures of the common as they lived their fragile, anxious lives.

The demon calf had given her food last night. Not in an exchange, even, but as a *gift*.

No strings attached, was the demon saying. But they lied. Oh, how they lied.

Edrin closed her eyes tight. Her head was beginning to throb, even though she was Tribe and Sia's song had no power over her. And with each heavy throb a new thought burst through her mind.

The demon calf sought me long.

It kept me in its mind.

It brought me food when I was starving.

It grasped me and did not kill me.

Edrin remembered its hot, strong grip. Its eyes, grey as a snow-laden sky. Its belly-quivering voice.

She opened her eyes and peered out through the barbed bars of her nest. Sia's song, thin and pure and deadly, had given the air a sickly look, green as poison.

When the demon calf's mind was melted, its memory would be lost. It wouldn't know anyone, wouldn't remember anyone. Everything that it had ever thought or felt would be gone, vanished, wiped away.

But at that thought violent hunger-pains suddenly gripped Edrin, and she was torn with the agony of a great longing, an unbearable yearning.

But it was not for food.

No. She could hardly believe it, but it was not for food.

She found herself crawling out of her nest into the grey afternoon. She didn't know what she was going to do. She wasn't even sure what she *wanted* to do. But she found herself chasing through the trees along the silver trail of Sia's deadly song.

Franz gazed at the water of the pool with wonder, though somehow without surprise. The pool had swollen up into a great glowing dome. Soon, he was sure, it would burst and he would be swept away on a great green wave.

That would be good. His head was full of itches and the water would soothe—

—*crack!*

Franz flinched massively and forgot the dome of the pool. Something had just bitten him, or stung him, or hit him. His knuckle was smarting as though—

—*crack!*

Ouch!

But what . . .

. . . but what . . .

Franz looked around, blinking, as if awakening from a dream. For a moment he thought he caught a glimpse of a tall silver woman sitting in one of the naked trees, but—his brain did an awkward backward flip and landed awkwardly—but just a minute! Just a minute, this was all wrong. *All* wrong. The whole place. The sky, and the shadows, and . . . hang on, yes, the sun was behind him, sending weak shadows across the pool.

Behind him?

But that couldn't be right because he'd only just—

—*ouch!*

Hang on a minute! Someone was chucking stones at him!

Franz shook his head to try to clear it, but he only succeeded in stirring up his brain into more muddy confusion. The horrible itching in his head wasn't helping him, either.

What was going on? Everything had been so beautiful

and soothing just a moment ago. The pool had swollen up into a lovely emerald dome, and—

—*ouch!*

That stone caught him on the ear, and that *really* hurt. Franz clapped his hand to the sting and whipped his head round.

Something was beckoning to him from the middle of a bush. Something white-haired, shaggy. It might almost have been a sheep.

Except that suddenly it bared its fangs and said, in a voice almost as shrill and pure as a shrew's:

Come!

26

'*Come,*' said the ice maiden. '*Come!*'

Franz blinked through the blue evening. The pool beside him had gone flat again, and the trees had ceased their swaying dance. But just a moment ago . . .

But never mind that, because here was the ice maiden plain before him.

'*Come,*' she said again.

He'd never seen her properly before, not in daylight. She was huge-eyed, and so thin that her skin fell into valleys between her fragile bones. One strap of her tattered silver dress (it was what the Squirrel would have called an evening dress) was hanging off her shoulder. That was all she seemed to be wearing, apart from a bracelet of beer-bottle tops.

'Why were you throwing stones at me?' he asked, too bewildered to know if he were more angry or afraid. His voice sounded deep and bellowing after hers.

She wasn't looking at him. She was looking so fixedly past his shoulder that he had to glance behind him to make sure there was no one there.

No one. Well, no one he could see. But he was almost

sure there *had* been someone else—someone tall—perhaps an ice *woman*.

His mind still felt oddly soft, though, and he didn't feel very sure of anything, as if he were in the middle of a dream of a dream of a dream of a . . .

'*Come!*'

The ice maiden turned her thin back on him and began to run; and Franz, still too muddled to be sure what was happening, scrambled to his feet, seized his coat, and started after her.

She looked as if she were moving at no more than a steady jog, but Franz could only just keep up with her. He was too busy ducking under branches and hurdling logs to worry about where she was leading him, but somewhere at the back of his mind he was vaguely aware of a small terrified voice screaming at him to be careful. Last time he had followed the ice maiden . . .

(. . . but why was it the evening all of a sudden? That was what he couldn't understand. Why was it . . .)

Quick, quick, she was getting ahead.

The ice maiden ran through the trees and into the shade of a dark stand of conifers. She dodged between them easily, gracefully, her long feet hardly seeming to touch the ground, and Franz lurched and panted after her as best he could.

By the time Franz had burst out of the gloom beneath the trees the ice maiden was so far ahead that she was hardly more than a glimmer through the trees. Franz stopped, swallowed, heaved in a huge breath or two, and threw himself on.

And then before he knew what was happening his stupid coat had tripped him and he'd gone flying.

He hit the ground, rolled, and ended up flat on his back gasping up at the spiky tree tops.

Damn!

The ice maiden would be far ahead by now. He'd have lost her.

Damn!

But then before he could move something thrust itself into view right above him and Franz jumped like a startled fawn. He stared up at the wild-haired silhouette. He could just make out the gleam of the ice maiden's green eyes against the dimming sky. They were gazing fiercely at the patch of mud beside his left ear.

'Fool!' it snarled. Its voice was painfully shrill and very angry. 'Why do you lie in the mud?'

Franz, winded and still very confused, wasn't sure where to start answering.

'I fell over,' he said.

The ice maiden's face was set in a grimace of suspicion and disgust.

'Are your bones broken?'

'I don't think so.'

The ice maiden showed a pair of shining fangs. Her silver gown was belted with a man's tie. There was an old kitchen knife tucked into the silken band.

'Are you dying?' she demanded, fiercely.

He pushed himself up cautiously on one elbow.

'I don't think so,' he said again.

She was on tiptoe, ready to flee, as uneasy as a grounded

hawk. Yes, she was very like a hawk, or a fox. Some creature both hunter and hunted. Franz had no idea what she was going do next. He wouldn't have been surprised if she'd drawn her knife and plunged it into his chest.

He could sending her flying with a kick. Or squirm to his feet and run and run.

But he'd waited too long for this: and anyway, she fascinated him.

'What are you?' he asked. His heart was beating fast with fear, but with exhilaration, too.

She turned her head a little more to the side, so her green eyes were fixed on the cream and burgundy stripes of the silver birch behind him.

For a moment the fierceness of her face faded. And she looked puzzled, almost bewildered.

'Hungry,' she said at last.

27

The scent of the demon rose up to Edrin's nostrils as it lay in the mud: its warm breath, its sweat, its faintly rotting coat, its sap-perfumed hair—foreign, fascinating, dangerous.

But it was its eyes that really frightened her. They watched her constantly. She kept her own eyes turned away, of course, but the air around the demon was boiling with slave-vines. She could sense them questing and coiling and trying to work their way through her thin skin.

(But why was this demon trying to enslave her, when it wasn't slave-bound to anyone else? When it had even withered the vines of the female demon who lived in its box-house?)

But never mind why, she had rescued the foul thing from Sia, and now she must get away at once. Flee from the demon's great dangerous eyes and deadly vines.

The demon spoke, sweet-toned as a wounded stag.

'I thought you'd be hungry,' it said. 'So I brought some food. Here.'

It had propped itself up on its elbow and it was delving in its bag. It brought out some of the flat white stuff it had given her before. She snatched it, darting forward and back again quickly so as not to let it get a grip on her. She crammed the stuff into her mouth, chewing at it sour-faced. She gulped it down even though the smell was sickening.

It watched her.

'I'm sorry it's only bread,' it said. 'I didn't have a chance to get anything else. Anyway, I wasn't sure I'd be able to find you.'

'You *didn't* find me!' she snarled, swallowing down the last of the stuff with an effort. It was odd, and perhaps it was because she had this revolting demon in front of her, but suddenly she found she wasn't hungry, after all.

The demon calf shivered, sat up, and began to slip its great arms into the sleeves of its coat.

'No,' it agreed. 'It's not easy when I can't always see you, so I thought I'd wait by the pool and hope you'd come along again. But I must have fallen asleep, I think.' Then it looked up sharply and she only just got her eyes away from its face in time. 'Hey, what were you doing throwing stones at me?'

She shrugged her thin shoulders. She knew she should be getting away, far away—but somehow she didn't.

'Sia was taking you in thrall,' she said.

'Who? In what?'

Oh, why did it keep *talking*? And looking and *looking*? And why was it trying to tie them together with slave-vines when it was tied to no one else? *Why?*

'No more!' she said fiercely. 'No more words. You shall not enslave me!'

The demon rubbed up the silly shaved hair at the back of its neck. Demons changed the fashion of their hair and clothes with every season, almost. But it was futile, for they remained always demons.

'It's just that I want to understand,' it explained at last. '*In thrall* . . . is that like being hypnotized? Because there was someone by the pool. A woman. Like you, a bit. Was that Sia?'

And then he suddenly looked up at her again and just for an instant their eyes met.

Edrin reeled back from the force of its gaze. For a moment she couldn't breathe. It was as if a tendril of some great plant had looped itself round her ribs. She let out a shriek of panic and such a blast of frozen fear that crystals of ice formed on the heavy vine.

And, frost-blasted, it withered.

She stood, gasping with shock. She'd thought she'd understood the demon slave-vines, but she'd never imagined anything as terrible as this.

The demon was holding its ears and shuddering down into its coat.

'You've gone even colder,' it said. 'Your eyes have frosted over.'

She must run and run and run and never go anywhere near a demon ever again.

But still, somehow, she did not go.

'Do not hold me in your gaze!' she spat. 'You shall not slave-bind me. Never! You are nothing to me!'

But the demon only stared at her even harder. It was as if it couldn't stop itself. She almost took her knife from her belt and killed it there and then.

'Then why did you rescue me from Sia?' it asked, as the

air between them grew thick with reaching vines.

'Because I hate Sia!' she spat.

The demon's eyes fell, then, thank all the stars.

'Yes,' he said, quietly. 'That's often why people do things.'

These demons were such fools, such fools. They made songs about these vines as if they were something marvellous. As if the vines that linked them together made them warm, safe, even happy.

And all the time the vines were shackling them together into a slavery which was more terrifying than death.

'But I don't think I'm very good at hating,' the demon calf went on, quietly. 'I've tried, but it's not . . . it's not what I *want*, to hate people. Sometimes it's even hard to remember not to trust them.'

She turned her head even more away from it. The demon's bag didn't look empty. Was there more food in it? It would be foolish to leave before she'd got all the food the demon had. Although . . .

She stopped and listened to her body. Definitely no hunger. None at all. No cold, either, even though her hands were covered in a fur of frost as fine as moleskin.

'Only fools trust,' she answered, still searching herself for the hunger which had been her companion for so long. 'Trust leads to blindness, and a blind man cannot hunt. That is why we must all live alone.'

But for some reason that word, *alone*, echoed strangely through her bones. But that was foolish because she'd always been alone. *Alone* was natural. She'd been alone for centuries. It was only during this last long winter that she'd become discontented, and so hungry that her skills as a hunter had not been enough to keep her strong. But now, at last . . .

And then a terrible understanding struck her. And suddenly she knew why she had saved this demon. And why she was here now, right here, even though being here was threatening her life.

It was only since this demon calf had come to the common that she had been hungry and cold.

And it was only now she was with it that her hunger and cold had gone.

She stood, aghast.

Her hunger had not been for food or warmth at all. Her hunger had been for something else. Something she did not have words to express. Something that she had only just found. Something perilous. Something deadly.

Her hunger had been pulling at her, teasing her, weakening her, imprisoning her for months: but it was for nothing she could hunt, nothing she could catch, nothing she could hold on to, nothing she could devour.

Her hunger was weakening her, and could never satisfy her.

'*So I must be dying,*' she whispered, through lips that were suddenly crusted with ice.

28

The ice maiden's eyes were blazing like green fire through the frost on her face. Yes, Franz could believe that she was dying.

'Let me help you,' he said, urgently, putting a hand on her cold arm. 'That's why I've come here, to help you.'

But she jumped away as if his hand had burnt her.

'No!' she spat, putting up her hands to show nails which were not nails at all but claws. 'You cannot! I am Tribe! I must be alone!'

'I understand that,' he said quickly. 'I do. It's been the same for me. My parents ... We used to live in Berlin, you see, and my mother and father ... '

Franz stopped. Clenched his fists. Went on.

'My parents don't believe in helping outsiders. People in Berlin don't. They believe in getting rid of people who are weak or different.'

'Yes!' snapped the ice maiden. 'The strong always destroy the weak and take their hunting grounds. But that does not matter for I shall be strong again soon. I am Tribe, and I *shall*! You have tainted my mind, but I am not slave-bound. I can free myself.'

Franz didn't understand half of this, and he wasn't sure if the other half was true.

Did the strong always destroy the weak?

He remembered poor Hans the match seller. And Frau Rosen.

'There was an old lady in Berlin,' he said suddenly. 'And sometimes when I was little she used to give me sweets. That's a sort of food. Very good food.'

The ice maiden was blinking, swaying uncertainly from one foot to the other. Through the dusk her skin looked blue-tinged and almost luminous.

'The old female was cunning,' she muttered. 'It was making you its slave. Demons are foul. Foul, and full of evil.'

'What? Oh no, Frau Rosen wasn't—'

'—it is true!' Her face was full of deep horror, but utter determination. 'It happened long ago, and yet you remember it. The old female enslaved you. But I shall be free. I *shall* be free!'

Franz shook his head.

'Frau Rosen was just being kind,' he said doggedly. 'Yes,' he went on, with a kind of amazement. 'She was being *kind*.' Talking to the ice maiden had made that clear at last after months of muddle. Frau Rosen had lived to be old—had survived to have grandchildren—but she'd always been kind.

'*Kind?*' the ice maiden spat, with contempt. She swung herself away from him and for a moment Franz thought she was about to run away again. '*Kind* is nothing. Only a tale in a song. It has no power.'

She sounded so certain that Franz wavered. Was that true? Had Frau Rosen only been cunning, and not kind at all? Only out for what she could get?

None of the clever grown-ups in Berlin had talked about being kind. Not kind to outsiders, anyway. Not to anyone weak. Franz had never heard anything much about kindness from the men in spider-sleeved coats who drove along in the bright parades, or the fat businessmen who came to the Wolf's parties.

Franz hunched himself down into his coat. These English were backward, of course, but would they catch up eventually with the Nazis' advanced way of thinking? Wake up, anyway, to the instincts that were running hotly under their skins. Would they band together and come hunting for him and the Squirrel? Come and smash all the windows of the house? Drag him into the street? Take him away?

It stood to reason that they would. Of course it stood to reason. But still . . .

But still, Frau Rosen had been kind, and she had lived happily for many years.

'I don't know why the old lady was kind,' he said, at last, exhausted with thinking. 'But she *was* kind, all the same. And that's why I've come to help you. Because if I don't, then the world won't be a place where I can live.'

And that was the heart of it, at last. He'd tried to learn to be like the Squirrel and the Wolf. But after all he had a choice.

Even if it was going to put him on the losing side with Frau Rosen, he had a choice.

He looked up and found himself staring straight into the ice maiden's green eyes.

She met his gaze for a second. Then she gasped hugely, as if he'd stabbed her, and before he had time to know what was happening she'd clapped her thin hands over her face, ducked away from him, and run.

He scrambled up and started to follow her, but he never had a chance. In a few darting seconds she was out of sight.

And even the chilly trail she had left behind her had dissolved into the twilight of the wood.

29

Franz stood alone in the increasing darkness of the wood. He hardly dared move, because the wood had suddenly gone taut with a terror which put eyes in every tree.

Something snickered through the leaf litter at his feet, a shrew or a vole, probably. There was no sign at all of the ice maiden. But still, he didn't think she was far away.

Franz walked forward a few steps, looking constantly around him through the multitudes of charcoal tree-trunks.

'Where are you?' he asked quietly.

It was getting dark and he should be on his way home. But he went on, anyway, following the path the ice maiden had taken.

It was the cold, as usual, that told him she was near.

She was lying on her stomach along a bough of an oak tree. Her green eyes were glaring down at him, fierce as a fox's.

'There you are,' he said, with relief.

She fixed him with a blazing stare.

'Of course I am here!' she hissed. 'I cannot be anywhere else. Your vines have caught me.'

'What?' said Franz, startled. 'My *what*?'

'I knew it would happen,' she went on, sourly. 'That is the demon way, to enslave all others with slave-vines. I withered those I could, but demons are cunning, and now you've pierced my bones.'

Franz hadn't the faintest idea what she was talking about.

'Demons?' he echoed, with alarm, looking around at the shadows of the wood. '*Demons?*'

She did not answer him, so he asked, again:

'What demons?'

She showed him her long icicles of fangs.

'*Demons,*' she spat. 'Are you too stupid even to understand that? *Demons!*'

'But ... what demons?' Franz asked, rattled and confused.

She gave her white rat-tails of hair a swift exasperated shake.

'Like the one you can see in the pool!'

Franz looked back hastily over his shoulder. He'd spent hours and hours sitting beside the pool. *Demons* sounded impossible, ludicrous. Fairy-tale things.

But if there were people on the common like the ice maiden ...

For a moment he imagined a demon: a great muscle-bound creature rising up from the water, weed dripping all around it. Rising higher and higher ...

The ice maiden hissed like a snake through her long white fangs.

'Fool! Clod! Demons are not over your shoulder or behind your back. Demon is *you*.'

Franz's view of everything suddenly turned inside-out.

A demon? Him?

A *demon*?

She had turned away from him again. Her skin glistened, highlighting the sharp bones of her skull. She was as delicate and fierce as a hawk. So what would *she* think of *him*?

He suddenly saw himself with her eyes, all heavy bones, and great muscles, and earth-shaking slowness.

Like an ogre.

Like a *demon*.

'But . . . I've never made anyone into a slave,' he said, tentatively.

She hissed again, turning her green eyes, tiger-fierce, straight into his.

'Then why am I here?' she demanded.

'Why—?'

'It's because you have pierced me with your vines,' she said. 'And so we are tied together.' She paused. Her face was closed and grim. Then she launched herself down from the tree and landed beside him as lightly as a robin.

'Why did you have to come here, day after day?' she demanded, bitterly, the green light of her eyes making everything round him seem suddenly much darker. 'You have been tainting my mind all winter. Poisoning it. And now you have enslaved me so I must be with you always.' She spat out a long glob of blue slime and Franz had to move his foot quickly to avoid it. 'But perhaps I shall kill you, instead,' she went on, darkly. 'Even though the vines between us will pull me into agony. Even though they might make me die, myself.'

Franz wondered for a second how on earth he'd got involved in this.

The ice maiden began to walk away from him back along the way they'd come.

He hesitated for a little while.

But then he followed her.

30

Sia climbed high into the whipping branches of a birch tree and scanned the twilight wood.

There it was. There was the demon calf. Stomping along, crushing delicate and delicious creatures under its great shoes as it went.

It had escaped her earlier, but it wouldn't escape her long. No, and neither would the foolish maid Edrin who had saved it.

There would be no way for Larn to find out how Edrin had died, after all.

There was the demon again. Sia could see its shining fawn-coloured hair. And beside it . . .

Sia took in a swift breath of danger.

That was Edrin's straggle of white hair.

Edrin was with it.

Edrin and the demon calf, together. Not just watching each other, but *together*.

Sia leapt swiftly down from the branch. The tatters of her skirts swirled around her like a sudden whirlwind as she jumped down to the ground.

This must be stopped before it put the whole Tribe into

desperate peril. The Tribe must not show itself plainly to demons. Why, demons had become so powerful that their monstrous machines could crush earth and trees together until the whole common was dead and the Tribe, bereft of their hunting grounds, died with it.

That demon must never return to the city to tell its tale, and Edrin must not show herself outside the common. But they were almost at the road, so what could be done? There was no time to sing the calf into a slow enthralment.

The demon must have an accident. It must be driven as far as possible from the common, but it must be dead before it reached its city.

And the maid Edrin must be stopped, too. Of course she must. Even Larn would agree. If Edrin went into the demon city the Tribe would be discovered. Demons had songs about the Tribe, of course, but one of the Tribe standing visible in their own city would rouse them to fear and hatred. And then they would hunt the Tribe and destroy them.

Sia was strong, but she could not be sure of killing both Edrin and the demon. She needed help to pin this quarry down. Sia turned full circle, searching for a scent of strength.

Then, not loudly, but in a voice that cut through the air like a hurtling, screaming swift, she called:

'*Tribe!*'

And the Tribe heard her.

31

The ice maiden halted so suddenly that Franz nearly fell over her.

'What's the matter?' he asked, for she had dropped into a crouch and was looking fearfully round at the darkening trees.

'What is it?' Franz asked again.

Her green eyes were wide and glittering.

'*Tribe!*' she replied, in the tiniest possible whisper.

'Tribe?' echoed Franz, puzzled. 'What's Tribe?'

She glared up impatiently, sending a ray of emerald light full into his eyes; but then she flinched and quickly turned her head away again.

'Sia is Tribe,' she whispered. 'I am Tribe.'

Franz looked around hastily. The woods seemed empty, but of course that meant nothing.

'Where are they?'

'Coming!'

The ice maiden got up and began to run, dodging purposefully through the clumps of dewy gorse. Franz gasped once or twice, but then set off after her.

'What do they want?' he asked, as he ran.

'They are hunting.'

'Hunting? Hunting what?'

'Me. You.'

'*What?*'

The ice maiden didn't answer. She ran on between the spiky gorse bushes into a belt of skinny trees, then out again onto more grey grass. She kept spitting *faster!* over her shoulder, but Franz was already running as fast as he could. He wouldn't be able to keep up this pace for long, either.

Her white rat-tails flicked her cheek bones as she turned her head.

'*Faster,*' she hissed. '*Faster!*'

Franz got his foot caught in something and nearly went head over heels. 'I can't *go* any faster!' he gasped, staggering and hopping and just saving himself.

She came to a dead stop, then, her head turning this way and that like a deer that scents danger.

'Then we cannot out-run them,' she said.

Franz put his hands on his knees and tried to get his breath back. For a moment, not running was such a relief it was hard to care about anything else.

'You could go invisible,' he gasped.

She turned to him with real anger.

'And do you think I could drag you with me all the way to the stars?' she snapped.

He had to guess what she meant.

'But *you* could go invisible,' he repeated. 'Then *you'd* be safe, at least.'

But she only bared her fangs.

141

'I cannot,' she said, furiously. 'Not now you have enslaved me. Your slave-vines are heavy. They weigh me down to earth, and I am weakened already through hunger. Such long, long hunger as you have caused me, demon.'

'So what can we do?' Franz asked. The trees were moving uneasily in the evening breeze, and every motion seemed to hide a shadowy figure.

The ice maiden let out a great shuddering sigh.

'Run,' she said; and took hold of his sleeve with an icy hand. 'It is hopeless. But all we can do is run.'

32

The ice maiden ran with the power and poise of a deer, and Franz pounded along as best he could beside her.

She led him downhill. They could go faster once they'd reached the road and were free of anthills and low branches, but all the time the air was getting colder, and Franz was wondering if the chill behind them was all due to the darkness that was weighing down the last sinking sliver of the sun. He was desperate to look behind him, but the ice maiden was clutching his sleeve in a fierce and fragile grip and he was afraid of cracking her bones.

So he kept his eyes forward, and she ran beside him like a silver shadow.

They were beside the sheep field when Franz first caught a glimpse of something moving alongside them on the other side of the overgrown hedge. The ice maiden must have seen it too, for her pace increased.

'No,' Franz gasped, almost falling on his face in his efforts to keep up. 'I can't—'

But now there was something visible through the hedge on the other side of the road, too: something shining faintly, like the moon through mist.

But it wasn't the moon. And there was no mist.

He found he could run faster, after all. He was running faster than he'd ever run before. Even the ragged catching of his breath and the pains in his chest didn't stop him.

'What are they?' he managed to ask, all in one swift precious gulping breath.

'*Sia! Tribe!*'

The Tribe people weren't far away. And they could run much faster than Franz.

The ice maiden suddenly let go of Franz's sleeve and plunged away from him into the hedge.

'Quick!' she spat.

There was a narrow gap between the scratchy branches. Franz threw himself at it.

The ice maiden was already well ahead by the time he'd barged his way through. He chased after her across a field of drenched rough grass. Her feet made so little noise on the ground that it was like following a ghost. Or perhaps it was Franz himself who was unreal, who was in some terrible dream, running and running surrounded by silent icy enemies. He found his skin itching, found himself expecting at any moment to feel the stealthy touch of the striding four-legged spiders.

But no, that was a different dream.

Look—over by the drooping willows—there was a figure that was somehow shadowy, even though it was gleaming with a pearly glow.

The ice maiden had seen it too. She made a tiny sound like a kitten's mew and then suddenly she was leaping the hedge beside her in one impossible, deer-like bound. For an instant Franz saw her silhouetted against the sky, all slender limbs and flying hair.

And then she was gone.

Franz charged into the hedge and fought his way through after a brief wild struggle. He came out into the boggy meadow which lay beside the river. The last light of the setting sun was etching every anthill and tuft of grass as sharp as ice.

A shrill sliver of sound came back to him from the running figure of the ice maiden.

'*Run!*'

So he ran—but very soon his shadow squirmed, and became a jerking criss-cross. There were two swift and glimmering figures not far away on either side of him.

The Tribe. Hunting.

Franz put all his strength into one last sprint for the bridge. For a few strides the grey figures on either side of him didn't seem to be getting any closer, and Franz felt a spark of hope.

But then he realized that was because he wasn't being chased any more. This hunt was no longer about the chase. He was being herded.

There wasn't time to work out where.

The soles of the ice maiden's long narrow feet were flicking up in front of him, grey as the dusk. She was nearly at the river and the shadows of the great alder trees seemed to be reaching out as if to grab her.

And then, absolutely suddenly, she staggered. She threw up a claw-fingered arm as if trying to fend off a blow; and then she went down on her knees.

Franz reached her in five heart-bursting strides.

'*What is it?*' he gasped. He would have shouted, but he didn't have the breath. They were only a hundred yards from the bridge, now, and over the bridge the town began, and with it perhaps some hope of safety. A few seconds' dash.

It was even harder to see now, because the ice maiden had fallen into the shadow of the alder trees, but her body had gone rigid and her mouth was locked open, as if in a silent scream. She seemed suddenly to be in such agony that Franz wasn't even sure she could hear him. He seized her arm to try to urge her on. She was lighter than he'd thought possible, but her legs didn't seem able to support her and he wasn't going to be able to drag her.

He looked round hastily. There were a dozen grey and gleaming figures only a little way away, now. They were no longer running, but walking calmly forwards, their limbs shining pale.

For a moment he was frozen by their beauty, like a mouse in a snake's gaze, but then he turned back to the ice maiden. She was hardly as heavy as a cat, but he couldn't run with her.

He shook her a little.

'Quick,' he pleaded. 'It's not far. Please, *quick!*'

And that must have got through to her, because all of a sudden her body convulsed as if someone had cut her with a lash. She rolled away from him, staggered somehow to her feet, and began to stumble away across the rough grass. She moved clumsily, awkwardly, as if she'd gone blind.

The silver figures stood and watched her. There were

women and men, all young and heart-stoppingly beautiful—but somehow at the same time as old as the river itself.

Then one of them—the tallest man, whose hair gleamed gold—raised an arm. And in the last rays of daylight Franz saw a something. A spear.

The ice maiden was still moving, staggering, one thin arm held up as if to protect herself. She was out of the shadow of the alders, now and she seemed to be reviving a little.

But it was no good.

The Tribe man threw hard, hard, and the spear flew from his hand, straight and true.

And struck.

It thudded into the ice maiden's pale back. Pierced her.

She let out a sound like a sigh, staggered, and collapsed. Went from life to crumpled stillness in an instant and dark blood bloomed from her back.

Franz couldn't believe it. He stood there aghast and couldn't, *wouldn't* believe it.

But she lay there and lay there.

And she didn't move.

33

And then the pale and gleaming eyes of the Tribe turned on Franz, and all he could do was run.

He cast one last despairing glance at the crumpled body of the ice maiden—

—and saw it move.

Not much. Not even enough to be quite sure, but—

—he flung himself down onto the drenched grass. The ice maiden was curled up like a child. The point of the spear, glistening with sticky darkness, was jutting horribly from her thin chest.

Her fingers were twitching a little, but her eyes were closed and her whole face was at rest, at peace, as Franz had never seen it. Franz was suddenly certain he was watching her die. She was leaving the earth and going to oblivion. Or heaven. Or the stars.

Suddenly he felt desperately alone. Desperately alone.

She had run, but not fast enough or far enough. Was that how it was, after all? Kill or be killed, fight or die, hunt or be hunted?

Franz set his teeth. All right, then. He'd be the hunter. And here was a weapon near at hand.

He reached out for the spear, but instead of grasping it his fingers passed right through the shaft and all he felt was a streak of deathly cold.

He tried again disbelievingly. And again, and again. He even tried forming his fingers round the spear and tugging it along its glimmering length.

But each time his hands slid away as if through nothing.

The silver figures of the Tribe were watching him, smiling.

'Why have you done this?' Franz demanded in frustration. 'Why have you hunted her? She wasn't an outsider. She was one of you. She's *always* been one of you!'

But for all the answer Franz received he might as well have been talking to the alders whose black cones hung down through the gathering mist.

The ice maiden lay unmoving, at rest, and suddenly he realized that she was beautiful.

That recognition struck him like a blow.

And she was suddenly important, too. Terribly important. She was not of his family, or his country, or his race, or even his species, and yet it was desperately important that she shouldn't leave him. Shouldn't leave him all alone in the world.

He pushed his fingers through her matted hair and turned her wild, icy head so her face was towards him.

'It's not real!' he said urgently to her still face. 'The spear, it's nothing. It's just cold air. It's not real!'

He took hold of her hand even though its chill sent him shuddering and wincing down into his coat.

'Don't go,' he said. 'Don't go. Don't go.'

The glistening figures of the Tribe people were approaching, but he ignored them because now something was happening. He didn't understand it, but he felt as if there were invisible ropes curling through the air all round him, wrapping themselves around his arms and his legs and the ice maiden's thin body, and even the silver shadow of the spear.

The Tribe people were very close, now: in a few seconds their hands would be on him, cold as death.

Franz bent close to the ice maiden's stone-white face and shouted, trying with all his strength to breach the little space and infinite distance which divided them.

'Ice maiden!' he yelled. 'Listen to me! The Tribe isn't really strong. This spear is just a shadow! So you can't be hurt. You can't be.'

But then a skeletal hand came down on Franz's shoulder and the ice-cold of it drove everything out of his mind but utter terror.

He dived away along the wet ground, rolling, his arms striking out madly at nothing: and then somehow he'd got to his feet and he was running, sprinting as fast as he could. And it was as if some great strength had come out of the ice maiden through the ropes which were binding them and the spear together, because he was running with a speed and poise beyond anything he'd imagined possible.

The Tribe people were chasing him, of course, but it was only a little way to the bridge, and at this miraculous speed—

—but he had forgotten the river.

★ ★ ★

It was suddenly at his feet, deep and green and swift. And his miraculous speed was so great that it was only the tug of the invisible ropes that allowed him to stop himself on the very edge of the bank.

But then there was a jolt, as if one of the ropes had snapped or pulled loose, and he lost his balance.

With one piercing cry, he fell.

34

The stars had come for Edrin.

She had often visited them in their realm, of course, but those had always been thin, stretched, breathless times. Not like this. This was glorious. Although her limbs were as heavy as marble, the stars surrounded her, crimson and gold and swirling sapphire, close enough to breathe the spices on their breath.

Close, close.

And singing.

The voices of the stars had been with Edrin all her life, chiming through wind and ice and Tribe Song. But here they were buoyant, floating.

Dancing.

Yes, she thought, filled with lightness and wonder. Dancing. The stars had come to take her, but they were not fighting. They had never been fighting. They were—

'*It's not real!*'

The sudden blaring of the demon's voice jolted her, and the stars went out. Terrified, falling through uncounted fathoms of darkness, Edrin made a huge effort and called the stars back to her so that their colours bathed her once more, and she was filled with a floating joy.

But then the demon voice came again.

'*The spear, it's nothing! It's just cold air!*'

And instantly the stars vanished again, snuffed out. *Gone.* She would have wept if she'd had tears to do it. She needed the stars. She *wanted* them.

'*Don't go. Don't go. Don't go.*'

Oh, oh, but this was demon-cruel. Now even the star-song was fading until it was no more than the chiming of the river. And she was this demon's slave, and even in death the stars could no longer reach her.

'*Ice maiden! Listen to me! You can't be hurt. You can't be.*'

But she was. She would have screamed out her anguish to the sky if she'd only had breath to do it. The stars had left her and she was stranded in the infinite blackness.

Everything around her was dark and she was alone.

Alone, alone.

Screaming silently as the light faded.

35

Along the river bank, a soldier looked up from where he was tying two prisoners to a tree.

'What was that?' he asked. He peered back along the river. The water was hazy under the gathering mist, but . . .

One of his prisoners cast off his invisible ropes and became Hughie Badrick again in the time it took him to stand up.

'That was a really big splash,' he said. 'Too big to be a fish. Did you see anything, John?'

'I'm not sure,' said John Coker, astonished to be distracted from an imaginary adventure by what might even be a real one. 'Let's go and have a look!'

He set off along the path, and Hughie ran after him.

The remaining prisoner sighed, then got fatly to his feet and into the dull shoes of Dick Wright once more. He'd lived long enough in this town to have lost almost all hope of anything interesting ever happening. Even the Kraut's dad never seemed to do anything much, no matter how long they spent watching him.

But standing here alone in the cold dusk was even duller than being with the others, so he jogged heavily after them.

John Coker was gazing over the gently rippling water.

'Can't see anything,' remarked Hughie, beside him. 'Cor, it isn't half freezing here all of a sudden. And it's ever so dark. We'd best be going home, John.'

But there *had* been something. John was sure of it. He watched the patterns of the converging ripples.

And as he did a paleness loomed up from the green depths of the water and then sank gently, gently down again without ever quite breaking the surface.

The cold current turned Franz over and sucked him down.

He found himself looking up as if through a dim green tunnel to a circle of midnight blue. Around its rim dark ropes undulated like snakes.

Snakes . . .

Some distant part of Franz's mind knew he had to act, lash out, fight for his . . . for his something or other. But the whole universe had slowed down so hugely that it was hard to believe there could be any hurry.

A string of silvery bubbles rose lazily, lazily into the circle of blue, wobbling and wavering and casting surprising gleams of light into the gloom as they went, and Franz found himself rising slowly after them.

And then there came a sound.

It was a raw nerve-scraping screaming that knifed through his brain—a despairing shriek that tied itself round him, and through him, and pulled him relentlessly up out of the cold and towards . . .

★ ★ ★

'There!' John Coker shouted, full of excitement and horror. 'There! There's someone in there!'

Dick came lumbering up.

'Have you found anything?' he asked, without hope.

'A body!' yelped Hughie, his hands flapping. 'It's a *body*!'

Dick stood for several seconds with his mouth opening and closing. Then he gave a great wail of dismay and turned and ran, howling.

'*Help!*' he bellowed. 'There's a body! *There's a body!*'

The screaming in Franz's head was agonizing, and it wasn't going away. Instead it was tightening around him, pulling him upwards.

And now there was a shadow distorting the edge of the dim green tunnel of water.

It was someone's head. Someone's face. It was . . .

. . . Franz's mind suddenly broke through his confusion and back into real life.

John Coker. It was John Coker. His enemy, John Coker. John Coker, only feet above him.

Franz's lungs were hot, bursting, threatening to explode any moment unless he could heave in a great long . . .

. . . but his limbs were tied up in the painful lines of screaming, and somehow frozen.

John tore off his jersey.

'Are you going in?' asked Hughie, hopping round him. 'Are you, John, are you going in? The weed'll pull you down, it will! My dad said. It'll wrap round your legs and drown you. John! John, perhaps you should wait!'

John hastily trod off his shoes and pulled his flannel shirt over his head. The shirt caught on his wrists, but he tugged at it frantically until the buttons popped off and released him.

'Crikey!' said Hughie, breathlessly. 'Look, there it is again! I think . . . hey, John, it's the Kraut!'

John sat down on the edge of the riverbank. The water was so cold it bit his calves, but he slid himself into the water before he had time to think about it.

He waded forward gingerly. The mud on the bottom was soft and dissolved strangely under his feet. He groped round with his arms, but found only the great weight of the gently moving water, and the sharp-edged reeds.

Nothing.

And nothing—

—and then suddenly *really* nothing—no bottom—and he was falling head first into the gloomy water. He thought about panicking, but quite honestly didn't dare.

Then something touched his leg. Something big, something heavy.

He grabbed down and got hold of a good handful of something. He squeezed his fingers round it and pulled it towards him.

A hand grabbed Franz's coat, and at its touch fear burst him into action. *They'd come to get him. At last, at last, they'd come to get him.*

He kicked out urgently, urgently, urgently.

John was concentrating so hard on holding on to the something that when it lashed out it didn't occur to him to let it go. It dragged him down further into the freezing darkness. It was almost too cold to feel or think down there, but John kicked out fiercely until his feet found the ooze of the bottom, and then he pushed himself upwards as strongly as he could.

He rose agonizingly slowly, but in the end John's head broke the surface. There was so much water in his nose and ears and eyes that to start with all he could do was snort and gasp and sneeze. It was a while before he even thought about wiping his hair out of his eyes so he could work out what was going on.

Hughie was jumping up and down on the bank yelping, *Here! Here! They're here!*

There were some men coming out of the darkness: men running along the riverbank towards them, throwing off their jackets as they came.

Rescue. That must mean rescue.

But all John cared about was breathing and breathing and breathing, and keeping hold of the Kraut beside him, who was breathing, too.

36

By the time the first of the men arrived, John had managed to tiptoe and flounder to the water's edge.

'It's the Kraut,' Hughie was saying breathlessly. 'It's the Kraut! He was right under the water for ages and ages. John saved him! John *saved* him!'

'Thank God for that,' said one of the men, rolling up his sleeves. 'All right, then. Let's get them both onto dry land.'

'Here we are, then, boy,' said a second man, to the Kraut. 'Take hold of my arm and we'll soon get you out of there.'

'Are there just the two of you in there?'

'Has anyone got a torch?'

'Steady!'

'Got him?'

'I think—yes, here we are. That's it. Safe and sound. You'd better sit down for a minute, boy. That's it, while we see to your friend.'

'Here's someone coming with a torch. *Over here!*'

'Hello? Someone said something about a—good grief, it's Franz! Franz—'

'What, is this *your* boy, Mac? Well, don't worry, he's all

right. He's just jolly cold and wet but he's all right.'

Now someone was holding out a hand to John as he stood shivering in the water.

'Come on, then, lad, let's get you out of there. That's it. That's it. There, you're quite safe now. Good heavens, we'd better get that vest off you, though, before you catch pneumonia. That's it. Good grief, your mother will have a fit when she sees the state this is in. It's hardly fit for a dishcloth.'

John tried to say something, but his teeth were chattering too hard. The man used John's vest to wipe the worst of the slime off him, and then someone was helping John put his shirt back on. And still all John could do was shiver and wonder what the Kraut's dad had been doing with all these English men.

Now someone else was arriving. A lady, still wearing her apron. Mrs Jeffreys, it was, from the Fox and Hounds.

'Here, I've brought some blankets,' she said. 'Here we are. Thank the Lord they're all right, poor kids. Here we are, love, let me hold this round you while you get those wet things off. There. That's better, isn't it. Now, Mildred'll be along in a minute with some nice hot tea.'

John held the prickly blanket shudderingly round him while one of the men helped him into his socks and shoes.

Then one of the figures in the darkness said:

'Is that John? John Coker? Hey, young John, what do you think you were doing messing about in the river?'

John looked up. It was very nearly dark, now, but that was certainly Mr Boyes who was in the choir at church.

Hughie piped up while John was still trying to get some words past his chattering teeth.

'John *saved* him! We heard a splash and we ran along— and then John jumped in and *saved* him!'

'And thank the Lord for that,' said Mrs Jeffreys, devoutly. 'The poor boy. He's German, you know. I've been feeling so sorry for him, going about all alone for all these months.'

'You saved young Mackintosh? Really, John? Well, that was jolly well done, wasn't it, sir?'

John pulled the prickly blanket more tightly round him. He really needed to go away quietly somewhere until his brain could catch up with what was happening. What was the Kraut's dad doing with these people? With Mr Boyes from church? Surely *he* couldn't be a German spy, could he?

'Very well done,' agreed the man called *sir*. None of them was wearing uniform, but there was definitely a brisk, military air about their way of speaking.

And John had a sudden, horrible feeling that he and Hughie and Dick might have got everything totally *totally* wrong.

Franz heaved in lungful after lungful of the rough-edged air. He needed to concentrate on breathing and breathing, but people kept talking to him, helping him up, helping him take off his wet clothes.

They've come to take me away, he thought again.

'Franz! Are you all right?'

But that was the Wolf. It was too dark to see him

properly, but that was his voice, and his scent of tobacco and Brylcreem and bay rum. He was putting his greatcoat round Franz's shoulders. It was still warm from the Wolf's body.

One of the other men spoke.

'We'd best get these boys in out of the cold. Will you be able to get your boy home by yourself, do you think, Mac?'

'Yes, we'll be all right,' said the Wolf. He put a hand on Franz's shoulder. 'We must be getting you back, Franz.'

But Franz was still too confused to move. He was sure he'd been in the middle of something incredible and terrifying—but it was as if the river had washed whatever it was clean from his mind.

He turned to look back along the tussocky grass of the meadow, because he was practically sure he'd left something there. But it was too dark to see anything, now.

'Franz,' said the Wolf, kindly. 'Time to go home, now, old chap.'

The others were moving off towards the bridge.

But now Franz had turned away from the orange glow of the town it had stopped being so utterly dark. There were even a few tiny diamonds of stars studding the sky. They shed just enough light for him to see . . .

'What on *earth* . . . ' murmured the Wolf, beside him.

The Wolf hurried forward a few steps and squatted down. He placed the back of his fingers against what he found there, as if to test its temperature.

Franz went forward too and saw the glimmer of a silver dress. Some straggles of wild white hair.

He began to shiver uncontrollably.

'What on earth's been happening here?' demanded the Wolf, but he was lifting up the still body of the ice maiden without waiting for a reply. 'We must get help,' he went on, getting to his feet. 'We'll take her back to the bridge house. They'll be able to call for an ambulance, and—'

An ambulance?

Franz gasped in a mixture of fear and a terrible hope. 'She's still alive?'

'Just about,' said the Wolf, curtly. 'Come on!'

The Wolf was nearly back at the bridge by the time Franz caught up with him. The glow from the first street lamp was sparkling the ice maiden's dress. Her head was lolling back limply, but there was enough light for Franz to see her face, and . . .

Franz gasped with dreadful horror. Under the ice maiden's thin skin the bones of her face were melting, softening, blunting. Her long fangs were beginning to dissolve, too, like icicles in the spring.

The Wolf glanced down at the burden in his arms—and what he saw brought him to an amazed halt.

'What in the world . . . ' he began.

And suddenly Franz realized that he had delivered the ice maiden into the hands of a terrible enemy.

'Who is she?' asked the Wolf, still frozen with astonishment.

'The ice maiden,' Franz whispered. He couldn't think of anything else to say.

The Wolf gazed down at the girl in his arms: at her long curved claws, from which acrid wisps of steam trailed into the still air; and at her torn bodice which was—Franz gaped in new amazement—which was no longer stained with her dark blood.

Her eyelids fluttered, and for a moment Franz thought she was waking up. But she only sighed, and moved her head a little so it ended up resting against the Wolf's shoulder.

The Wolf looked at Franz.

'Where has she come from?' he asked quietly.

That was hard to answer, too.

'The woods,' Franz said.

The Wolf nodded, as if that made some sort of sense.

'She is a Gypsy, then.'

'No,' said Franz, quickly. 'She is . . . '

But he knew no word for what she was.

The Wolf shook his head. Then he sighed.

'Come on, Franz,' he said. 'I think we'd best all be getting home.'

37

Edrin opened her eyes. The darkness around her was bobbing about strangely; and the quietness around her was odder still. She couldn't hear so much as the fluttering of a wind-breathed leaf, or the creak of a dry branch, or the chiming of the stars. Not anywhere.

All she could hear was the sharp tapping of . . .

. . . *something* . . .

. . . and a scent of . . .

Edrin, baffled, tried to float away into a new dream, but she found herself tethered annoyingly to this one. So she woke herself up properly and looked around.

She was in a demon street.

A *demon street?*

By all the stars, *she was in a demon street!*

And here in front of her was a demon door.

And there, very close above her, was a demon face. An adult male, very close.

Very close.

She let out a scream and lashed out wildly. The demon's powerful hands clutched at her, but she fought it with all her strength and it couldn't hold her. She slithered down out of its arms in panic-stricken flailing stages and ended up on the cold stone just as the demon door opened and flooded the street with sickly light.

A female demon's anxious face peered out at her.

'*Alex? Franz? Was ist los?*'

Edrin gasped. There were demons all round her, looking at her. *Looking at her!*

The stars! Call on the stars! Quick, quick!

But the stars did not hear her.

38

The bedraggled and shaking girl on the doorstep was truly filthy—worse than the foulest tramp Franz had ever seen—and Franz waited for the Squirrel to patter fearfully back into the house and slam the door in the girl's face.

But instead the Squirrel smiled a timid smile which was quite unlike anything that had touched her frozen face since she had come to England. And then she reached out a hand towards the ice maiden, as if to a nervous dog.

'Will you come in?' she asked.

The ice maiden flinched away violently from the Squirrel's hand, but she stayed crouched on the wet doorstep. She was trembling. The wind was shiveringly cruel, but it was more than just the cold that was affecting her. She was paralysed with terror. Her green eyes darted round, as if looking for a way to escape.

And then they found Franz.

Franz didn't know what to do. Everyone had changed so utterly—the ice maiden, John Coker, the Wolf, and now the Squirrel—that he no longer felt sure of anything.

The Wolf put a hand on Franz's shoulder. 'Come along, then,' he said quietly. 'We must get you both warm and dry.'

Franz, still utterly confused, stepped carefully round the ice maiden and into the house. The ice maiden crawled in after him, her frightened eyes flickering everywhere. Her long feet kneaded the bristly doormat the way a cat's might.

Yes. The ice maiden had lost her fangs and claws, and her eyes were no longer sending shafts of light into the shadows. She was more like a human than she had been; but she was still rather like a cat.

The Wolf stepped in softly behind her, but as soon as he began to close the door she leapt round, teeth bared and her knife in her hand.

Franz took in a breath of horror—but the Wolf only sighed, and very slowly and gently took the knife away from her.

'It's all right,' he said. 'This isn't a trap. The door won't be locked. Look, if you turn this handle it will open again. See?'

The ice maiden looked from the Wolf to the door to Franz. Then she blinked, and nodded once, and backed into the room as delicately as if it were carpeted with shards of glass.

She was clothed in nothing but a straggle of sequined rags. Her thin legs were caked with mud, and her hair was matted and filthy. But mostly what Franz noticed about the girl were her eyes, her slanting fierce green eyes. They were no longer glowing like emeralds, but they were bright and silver-flecked and extraordinary all the same.

She went and squatted beside the fire, her hands on the rug as if ready to spring. Her eyes were darting constantly from one object to the next, and with each gloomy picture, or curtain, or comic dog ornament she saw in the rented house she flinched a little, as if their ugliness hurt her.

'I don't think she's been in a house before,' Franz explained, hesitantly. 'She's always lived on the common. But she can't live there any more. The people there don't want her.'

The Squirrel looked at him. And it was as if she understood, even though she couldn't possibly understand.

'She is a refugee, then,' she said.

'Yes,' agreed Franz, awkwardly. But then he thought about it and said: 'Yes. Yes, I suppose she is.'

The Squirrel nodded.

'Then we must care for her,' she said.

39

Edrin squatted by the flickering fire. Everything had changed. *Everything.* Every sight, smell, sound, rattled into her brain in a completely new way.

Perhaps these demons had stolen her mind. They were cruel enough. Why, this calf's terrible vines had pulled her away from the realm of the stars, and there could be nothing more terrible than that.

Edrin dug her claws fiercely into the woollen mat—but even that felt wrong. She glanced down, and then froze in new and dreadful terror.

Her hands! She had no claws—no, none at all. She had strange rounded fingertips and . . .

. . . she let out a mew of despair. She was so much changed. What she had been had almost vanished. Her skin, her very bones were hotter. Heavier. They weighed her down into the ground.

'No,' she whispered. But the word buzzed in her throat, came out in a growl.

The female demon was coming towards her. It was holding a woollen sheet, but it stopped when Edrin bared her teeth at her.

'For you,' said the female demon, timidly.

And this demon had changed, too. It could surely no longer even be a demon, for instead of being massive and hot she was small and slender, almost bird-like. And the male demon had changed, too—gone long and angular, with a sad, watchful face.

Edrin hunched her shoulders, trying in some impossible way to shrink away from her own body.

'Franz,' said the female demon, who was no longer a demon at all. 'You give her the blanket. Perhaps she will take it from you.'

Franz.

The girl had never considered the calf might have a name. She turned to inspect it.

And he wasn't a demon, either. He, too, had become some other creature, grey-eyed and pale. She looked at him and looked at him. Recognized him. And through her new heavy body some strange and thrilling certainty began to quicken her breath.

Suddenly she understood all those demon songs.

And she knew she was enslaved for ever.

But also, strangely, free.

40

On the whole, Franz decided, it was rather as if they'd let a wildcat in the house. A very large and powerful wildcat. Which swore a lot.

Though the girl *stank* more like a ferret.

They were plainly going to have to put up with the stink for the time being, though, because it was too late in the day to start heating the copper for baths. In any case, the girl recoiled from hot water with as much disgust as if they'd offered her a steaming chamber pot.

In fact she bared her teeth at anyone who came within a metre of her.

'But I am afraid she is hungry,' said the Squirrel, anxiously.

'I'm *sure* she's hungry,' said Franz. It was about the only thing he *was* sure of at that moment.

In the end the Squirrel left a plate of bread and jam on the floor just out of spitting distance.

The girl pounced on the plate as soon as the Squirrel had backed away; but then she looked up at Franz, her nose twitching suspiciously.

'Poison?' she demanded. Her voice was high and pure, like the voice of a thrush.

'No,' Franz told her. 'No poison.'

And at once her filthy hand shot out. She squeezed the jammy bread into an untidy ball, and she began licking neatly with a narrow pink tongue at the jam which oozed between her fingers.

And still neither the Squirrel nor the Wolf called for the police or the army. Not even when the girl pinched up a gobbet of crimson jam that had fallen on the rug and dropped it swiftly into her stained mouth.

Franz looked at the Wolf uncertainly, but the Wolf only shrugged.

'What's her name?' he asked.

And Franz found he didn't know. He wasn't even sure she *had* a name.

But the girl glared up at him with fierce silver-glinting eyes.

'I am Edrin,' she said.

Once Edrin had licked her hands clean (well, clean of jam, in any case) she crawled quickly under the table. She seemed to feel safest there, so the Squirrel stopped panicking about the lack of a spare bed and put a couple more blankets nearby.

Edrin snatched them, screwed them up, curled up on them, and appeared to go to sleep.

Franz put his chair under the door handle of his room again when he went to bed that night.

He dreamed of spiders, and spears, and soldiers' footsteps.

41

The Wolf had gone out by the time Franz got downstairs the next morning.

'With his coat stinking of the river,' said the Squirrel, ruefully. 'Franz, there is hot water ready for a bath.'

Franz certainly needed a bath—though not as much as the ice maiden—the girl—no, as *Edrin* did.

'I don't think Edrin's done much washing,' Franz told his mother, diffidently, when he'd got himself clean. He was listening all the time for the troop of soldiers the Wolf would surely bring to take Edrin away.

Surely he would. Surely.

Edrin did bare her teeth at the sight of the Squirrel's hot water. But this time the Squirrel only gave a tremulous smile, and held out the bottle of shampoo for the girl to sniff.

'This is to make your hair shine,' the Squirrel told her.

That caught Edrin's attention.

'A demon spell?' she demanded, in her piercing voice.

'In a way,' agreed the Squirrel, surprisingly. 'It works with the help of this hot water.'

Edrin peered into the bowl, sniffed dubiously at the steam, recoiled, sniffed again.

'How does it work?' she demanded.

The Squirrel smiled again, almost naturally. Almost genuinely.

Franz had to remind himself he couldn't trust her.

'The hot water must swirl through your hair a hundred times in a clockwise direction,' she said.

'Clockwise?'

'Like this,' said Franz, demonstrating.

The girl nodded, business-like.

'*Deasil*,' she said. 'It is star magic, then. And it will truly make my hair shine?'

'Truly,' said the Squirrel. 'You will be beautiful, Edrin.'

Edrin looked suddenly even more doubtful.

'It must be powerful magic to make me beautiful,' she said. 'Will it cause much pain?'

'Yes,' said the Squirrel, unexpectedly. 'Great pain, if you do not keep your eyes tight shut.'

Edrin sniffed at the shampoo again, looked warily from Franz to the Squirrel, and then nodded again.

'Very well,' she said, and plunged her head into the bowl, causing a tidal wave which flooded a considerable portion of the kitchen.

The Squirrel leapt out of the way. And then she suddenly laughed.

These demons had so much. So many possessions. Everywhere, everywhere, so much of everything. Clothes, fire, even *food*. Yes, they had whole planks piled high with food, which they kept behind doors which did not lock.

And not only did they have it, but they *gave it away*. Gave it to her, Edrin, a stranger.

So. That settled it, then. These demons were insane. Or, at least, if there *were* some rhyme behind their reason then Edrin did not understand it.

But then there was little here she really understood.

So she did the sensible thing. When her hair had dried she ate everything the female gave her. Then she visited the turd shelter. And then she curled back up on her wool-sheets again and went to sleep.

It was daylight, after all.

42

By the time the Wolf got home that evening Edrin had begun to smell relatively civilized. In fact Franz had almost forgotten just how thin and fierce and strange she was until he saw the shock on the Wolf's face at the sight of her.

To be fair, though, the shock was partly due to the fact that it was only when the Wolf sat down at the table that he discovered that Edrin was squatting underneath it making faces at herself in a hand mirror. And it didn't help, either, that Edrin was only wearing the Squirrel's laciest petticoat, her own bottle-top bracelet, and a furry golden tablecloth.

Franz had been waiting all day for the soldiers to arrive to take away this invader of the Wolf's territory. But none had come.

Edrin consented to sit at the table to eat her supper. She squatted on her chair, sheltering her plate with a skinny arm and glaring round ferociously between mouthfuls.

Franz was so completely confused that he could hardly think straight enough to eat. He still had no idea why on earth the Wolf and the Squirrel had let Edrin into the house. Edrin did seem to be much more human now—physically, in any case—but she was still much more of an outsider, much more different, much less *evolved*, than anyone else you could possibly imagine.

So why hadn't the Squirrel slammed the door in her face? And, for that matter, why hadn't the Wolf left her to die on the wet grass of the meadow?

Franz kept remembering Berlin.

The Wolf was definitely on edge. He kept clearing his throat; and when something came through the letter box he seemed glad of an excuse to leave the table.

Edrin snatched the Wolf's piece of cake from his plate as soon as his back was turned and crammed as much of it into her mouth as she could.

The Wolf came back opening a buff-coloured envelope. His face tightened when he saw the signature on the letter inside.

'What is it?' the Squirrel asked, quickly. But the Wolf had already turned back to the beginning of the letter. He got to the end, paused for a second, and then turned back to the beginning again.

Franz picked up the envelope. It had a German stamp, and the postmark was *Berlin*.

Edrin jumped off her chair and went to squat in the corner. Only Franz noticed that she'd taken the honey pot with her. She turned her back on the others and began scooping gloopy fingerfuls into her mouth.

'What does it say?' asked the Squirrel. She'd asked twice before, but the Wolf had shown no signs of hearing.

The Wolf got to the end of the letter again and drew

in a long deep breath, like someone who has just come up from deep water.

'They need some more information,' he said.

That might not have meant anything, except that the Squirrel had gone so still and so white.

The Wolf was reading the letter through yet again, but he roused himself to say:

'They want to know when I shall be back in the city, too. I shall have to write to them this evening.'

Franz looked from one to the other of them. He still didn't understand what was going on, but there was something new about the way they were talking. All the careful pauses and secret looks had gone.

Why?

'And *must* you go back?' faltered the Squirrel.

The Wolf looked up from the letter. Then he wiped his hand wearily down his face.

'Oh my dear,' he said. 'I'm so sorry.'

The Squirrel closed her eyes for a moment. Took a deep breath. Nodded.

'Of course,' she said bravely. 'Of course you must go back. And of course it will be quite safe for you. It is foolish to worry.'

Safe? But why should the Squirrel be worried about the Wolf being *safe*? The Wolf was a member of the Nazi Party. He had many important friends. If anyone were safe in Berlin it would be the Wolf.

There were just so many things Franz didn't understand. For a start, why had someone in Berlin written to ask the Wolf for information (*more* information)? What sort of information? And why had the Wolf been spending so much time at the bridge house, with the sort of British people who would run through the evening at top speed to try to save a stranger from drowning? Why had Franz and the Squirrel left Berlin in such a hurry and stayed away so long? And, most strangely of all, why had the Squirrel and the Wolf taken in Edrin, when the Wolf, at least, knew very well that she wasn't even properly human? That was the last thing a Nazi should do.

Franz held his breath. These new questions were bumping into all his old ones, and they had all begun drifting slowly but inexorably into new positions in his mind: and he was suddenly terrified of what they would reveal once they'd reached their new places.

But there was only one way they would fit together. Yes, only one way. And that meant . . .

. . . and that meant that for months and months he'd been almost completely wrong about very nearly everything.

'You're British spies,' he said, at last, in utter amazement. 'All the time you were giving parties and being friends with the Nazis, you were actually . . . '

He thought back to his last night in Berlin and found he understood what had happened then, too. 'The night before we left,' he said. 'Some people came to the door and you took them in.'

The Squirrel put her hands to her throat.

'I should not have done it,' she said, unhappily. 'It has caused so much difficulty, and in the end it saved no one. But Father was out, and I . . . I could not turn them away, Franz. The crowd was after them, and they were desperate.'

'But someone saw you let them in,' Franz went on, still working it out. 'And that was why the crowd came and attacked our house.'

The Wolf nodded, grim-faced.

'We didn't have much time to decide what to do,' he said. 'We've made ourselves well-known as supporters of the Nazi Party, and so obviously the last thing we should have been doing was sheltering anyone. But the city was full of crowds that night, and everything was confused. There was a fair chance that no one who mattered would find out exactly what had happened. At the same time, staying was obviously a great risk. In the end we decided that you and Mother should come to England for a holiday, and that I should stay on in Berlin.'

'Because you had to keep the business going,' said Franz, still not quite allowing himself to believe what the Wolf was telling him.

The Wolf gave Franz a searching look; and suddenly something inside Franz jolted, as if the Wolf had somehow caught hold of him.

'No,' said the Squirrel, earnestly. 'Not because of the business. Not because of the house, either. Because Father has built up a position where he can be of great use. Because we want to do everything we possibly can to help all the people the Nazis are planning to hunt down and destroy.'

A thin hand came up over the edge of the table and snatched the butter dish. They all saw it, but none of them took any notice.

'But . . . but how could you let me think you supported

the Nazis?' demanded Franz, in rising anger. 'How could you let me think you agreed with what they stand for?'

The Wolf sighed.

'We told ourselves that you were too young to question things,' he said. 'Anyway, we had no choice: we weren't allowed to tell you what was going on. All we could do was try to keep you away from the worst of it.'

Franz looked at the Wolf, who was perhaps not the Wolf at all. 'And so all the time you've been spending at the bridge house . . .'

'You need to forget all about that, Franz.'

But Franz was still testing things in his mind.

'But you've told me now,' he went on. 'So that means . . . that means I'm not going back, doesn't it. I'm never going back to Berlin.'

The Squirrel tried to smile.

'Well, England is perhaps not so very bad,' she said. 'And it will be easier, I think, now we have decided that you and I should stay. It has been hard to see you so lonely and unhappy, Franz. To feel that you hated us. I am glad that you have found out so much for yourself, so that now we must tell you the rest.'

But still Franz couldn't quite allow himself to believe them.

'If there's a war,' he said to the Wolf. 'If there's a war, will you really leave the house and the business and everything? Leave Berlin altogether?'

The Wolf looked taken aback, almost angry.

'Do you imagine I'd do anything else?' he asked. 'Do you think I'd stay to help the Nazis? Hunt down anyone that crazy system has decided is inferior to themselves? Do you think I'm an animal, Franz?'

Franz took a deep breath.

'No,' he said, with a dawning sense of wonder. 'No, I don't.'

43

After Edrin arrived nothing was ever the same again. It was like living with a whirlwind, or a tiger, or an unexploded bomb.

'Or possibly a Roman candle,' suggested Father, who was busy making arrangements for his return to Berlin. 'Shocking explosions, interspersed with awful pauses.'

Franz smiled, though to tell the truth there hadn't seemed to be that many pauses of any kind when it came to living with Edrin.

At least it was easy to explain Edrin's arrival to the many, many neighbours who called at the house after news of Franz's adventure in the river got around (and Mrs Jeffreys at the Fox and Hounds saw to it that the news *did* get around).

'She is a *Kindertransport* child,' Mother explained to everyone who asked.

The *Kindertransport* was a scheme where people in danger in Nazi countries could send their children abroad to safety.

'People seem very kind,' Mother told Franz, disconcerted but rather encouraged. 'Though,' she went on, looking troubled again, 'people must be the same everywhere, I suppose.'

'It's all right,' said Franz. 'Don't worry. Most people just follow the herd, and here the herd is running in a different direction.'

In any case, the *Kindertransport* was a good cover-story (*and it is true, after all*, said Mother, *for what child has travelled further?*) because everyone immediately felt very well-disposed towards Mother, very sorry for Edrin, and prepared to accept some odd foreign behaviour from both of them.

Though as far as Edrin was concerned *odd* hardly began to cover it. She was a serious embarrassment. For one thing telling the truth and politeness were totally foreign concepts to her, and for another she saw no reason why she should not steal anything she liked, especially if there was someone she could blame for the crime.

'Franz took it!' she would proclaim, when Mother yet again found some vital ingredient for supper missing.

And that with her mouth all smeared with treacle or dripping or whatever.

On the odd occasions that Edrin stopped causing mayhem for a moment, she was generally to be found standing pushed as far into the ivy on the garden wall as she could, her green eyes gleaming out through the jagged leaves as she chewed on heaven-knew-what.

'I think we need a proper garden,' said Mother.

Now they had Edrin they needed to move into a rather bigger house, anyway. The house they found was further from the river, and Edrin felt safer there. She would sometimes even venture out into the street as long as there was no cold wind which might hide the approach of one of the Tribe.

Franz could not, of course, risk Edrin going out alone in case she strangled someone or ate someone's kitten, and so he was forced into the company of the townspeople. It helped that John Coker, having saved Franz's life (more or less) and having also been the object of a thrilling lecture from the local police sergeant on the subject of National Security And Keeping Your Trap Shut, took a proprietary interest in him. What made things easier still was that Franz, while foreign and still wearing not completely the right clothes (though luckily his blasted coat had been completely ruined in the river) was quite boringly normal compared with Edrin.

Edrin would climb onto anyone's roof to retrieve a ball, and could bark at even the most terrifying dog in such a way that it rolled over and begged her to scratch its stomach. She could stalk and catch pigeons with her bare hands, and throw stones right over houses hard enough to break windows in the next street. She was extremely ready to use her new voice at the highest possible volume, too, which meant she soon got to be quite well known in the next *district*.

And if anyone dared to call Franz *Kraut*, or *Nazi*, then Edrin would turn on them, eyes blazing and quite probably with a sharp stone in her hand.

'Frank is *mine*!' she would snarl (no one in England seemed willing to say *Franz*, but that was actually something of a relief). 'He hunted me, and now we are bound for ever with slave-vines. Leave him alone!'

'For ever?' jeered someone, at last, greatly daring. 'Are you going to get *married*, then? You and Frank?'

Franz got ready to pull Edrin away from yet another fight to the death. But she was impossible to predict. Instead of launching herself into a vicious and skilful attack, she nodded with alarming smugness and certainty.

'Yes. That is how it will be,' she said. 'When we are full-grown we will be married and stay and make our own territory and hunt together for ever.'

That evening Franz asked Father about the possibility of going away to boarding school. But it was too late to get a place, apparently.

'And anyway, Mother will need you,' Father said.

So Franz stayed, and guarded both Edrin and the townspeople from harm.

He felt appalled and trapped and embarrassed and resentful and terrified.

But slightly fascinated, too.

44

Sia walked through the dancing light of the woods. Her silver gown had once swept the ground, but now, torn by bramble and rose, it danced and swirled round her in a hundred floating ribbons.

Sia came to the pool and leaned forward so she could see her reflection in the faintly quivering water. She had been beautiful for two thousand years, but her loveliness still delighted her.

Edrin's death was a cause for delight, too. The maid was out of Larn's sight, and the demon city would learn nothing of the Tribe, thank the stars, for demons with their snagging vines were cunning hunters. But now the demons would not be frightened and tempted into battle by the splendour and beauty of the Tribe.

Good. The common had long been Tribe hunting territory and now it would remain so.

Sia smiled at her white reflection. Edrin had long been a nuisance, anyway, as calves often were, whining and trailing and begging. The infant Sia had herself calved was no better, curse it. And when calves began to grow they could become rivals, as well as annoyances.

Unless you were careful.

Sia smiled, and her cruel fangs sparkled in the spring sunlight. Larn would soon forget Edrin.

A little way away a blade of grass twitched, and Sia froze, suddenly alert. Look, there! A polecat's foolish face, peering through the reeds.

Meat.

Sia dismissed Edrin from her mind and got ready to spring.

Everything about Edrin's life had changed. Everything. Even *time* seemed to have tied itself up in knots. Each human day was cluttered and dashing; but a human year seemed to stretch for nearly as long as a Tribe century.

But then the spring burst frantically into summer just as it always had. When Edrin had arrived on Frank's doorstep the trees were almost bare, but before even a week was out the hedgerows were punctuated with explosions of white may blossom.

And no sooner had the may begun to shatter than the cherry trees were offering their pink-and-white flowers to the sky.

Edrin went to the railway station with Frank and Auntie Hilda to see Uncle Alex off on his long journey to Berlin. The engine roared along like a midnight storm, but Frank had explained that it was stuck to its shining rails, so she did not try to fight it.

But when the train's doors were slammed and the engine began to hiss and chuff and rattle away Frank suddenly turned horribly pale, as if he'd got stomach ache from eating a whole basketful of raw potatoes, and started running. Running, running, after the train.

He ran right to the end of the platform. It was just as if Uncle Alex was pulling him along on a string, which of course he was. And then Frank waved and waved until the train had travelled the long curve and had wheezed its way out of sight.

Equally of course, Edrin found her guts burning with rage and jealousy. It was terrible, this being a demon—a *human*, that was what she must call herself, a *human*. It would be foolish to kill Frank because she was slave-bound to him. It would be almost as foolish to kill Uncle Alex, even though he took Frank's attention away from her. All these slave-vines caused nothing but mess and complication.

Still, she must keep alert and not give up her prey for anything. Not for *anything*.

'He will be back,' said Auntie Hilda, bravely. She was talking about Uncle Alex, of course. Though Auntie Hilda was only an earth-bound demon who could know nothing of the future, so was lying.

Edrin spent a lot of time in the new house sitting on the sill of her bedroom window gazing across the town at the slope up to the common.

'Let's go and see how the tadpoles are doing,' suggested Frank, one day. Demon memories were short, and Edrin had already realized that it was beginning to seem to him as if Sia and the Tribe were no more than dreams.

Edrin shook her shining white head as she viewed the great far-away trees. The common was continuing to grow and flourish even though she was not there to see it. And in the woods the mistle thrushes would be tenderly raising a new brood: tasty fledglings that would crunch in her mouth like crackling. Though raw meat gave her gut-ache, now, and she could no longer sick up feathers neatly.

'There is no need to go to the common,' she said flatly. 'Auntie Hilda has plenty of food for us here. Better food than pollywoggles. Anyway, Sia will be on the common. And the rest of the Tribe, too. It is not my territory any more for I am not Tribe.'

Frank hesitated.

'But the Tribe have already hunted you,' he pointed out. 'And I saw a Tribe spear sticking right through your chest. So they can't really hurt you, can they? Because when you woke up you were all right.'

She bared her teeth at him. She was glad to see it still scared him almost as much as it had when she'd had fangs.

'Of course the spear hurt me!' she snapped. 'It turned my veins to ice, and the stars came to carry me away. But you were shouting and shouting, and the slave-vines . . .'

Frank heaved a great sigh.

'You're always going on about slave-vines,' he said, for though he was certainly scared of Edrin, he was bold, too. 'But there *aren't* any slave-vines. You're a human yourself, now, more or less, and you must *know* there aren't.'

She nearly punched him out of pure exasperation; but he was getting pretty fast (or she was getting slower) and so starting a fight with him was getting increasingly risky.

Instead she sighed, too.

'Oh, slave-vines are true,' she said. 'You used them to bind me to you in the woods, and then when the Tribe tried to send me to the stars you used the slave-vines to pull me back to you, right from within reach of the stars. Back and back, down into this city of demons.' She shrugged her thin shoulders. 'So I shall never be free again. I shall never return to my home. I shall never hear the stars, or see them dancing. Because I am not alone any more, and I am not Tribe.'

Frank gave up even trying to understand her. She felt him do it. Felt the distance between them, as well as the vines.

'Neither of us shall return to our homes,' he said.

45

By the summer Franz was sometimes managing to forget where Edrin had come from. They were both at school by then. Mother listened to the news on the wireless every day and looked grave and worried. Everyone was talking of war.

Edrin did not understand it at all.

'But Frank will not let me kill my enemies at school,' she said, 'and yet you demons talk all the time of killing those too far away to know.'

Franz wanted to laugh, but didn't quite dare. Edrin was still fierce and sudden and lightning-quick.

'We may *have* to fight,' he explained. 'The Nazis believe they are the best sort of people, and that the world will be a better place if they kill everyone else. They want to move into our territory and take it over. They want to take over the whole world. But,' he added, hastily, 'it's all wrong that they're better than everyone else.'

Edrin looked relieved.

'Then they will not win a war,' she said, and might have added *QED* if she'd been even faintly interested in her school work. (Her Latin was fairly fluent, as it happened, though of a monkish variety. On the other hand she annoyed her teacher very much by rolling her eyes at his pronunciation of Shakespeare's verse.)

'Er . . . well, not necessarily,' said Franz.

But then of course Edrin flew into a rage.

'Yes, *necessarily*!' she snapped. 'It is the way of things. It has always been the way of things. The best, the strongest, survive and the weak perish. The weak cannot maintain their territory. They get hunted and killed. It is natural. It *must* happen.'

Mother opened her mouth and then smiled rather nervously and shut it again.

'But it's not *human*,' Franz told her, suddenly as passionate as Edrin. 'With all the other creatures in the world, yes, it's true, the strongest survives. But it doesn't work with us.'

Edrin stared at him fiercely for a moment. But then her face cleared.

'Because of the slave-vines,' she said.

Franz tried vainly to spot a connection, but Mother nodded.

'Yes,' she agreed. 'Because of the slave-vines. We humans use them to weave together a web of all our strengths, and it is stronger than anything else in the world.'

'A web of all your weaknesses, too,' said Edrin, with resignation and some disgust.

Mother frowned thoughtfully.

'Perhaps,' she said. 'Yes, perhaps sometimes our weaknesses bind us together even more powerfully than our strengths.'

Franz thought about Edrin, and his parents, and John

Coker, and all the people of the town. About the slave-vines that perhaps existed after all, and about the Nazis who wanted to hunt down and destroy everyone who was different. And he remembered the common; the long winter when he'd been truly alone. The sadness and loneliness and fear of it. The peace. The freedom. He remembered the creatures of the common: hawk and stag and beetle. Their savagery. Their beauty. The hunters and their prey.

Not far away through the window the common lay, lush and lovely and curling towards midsummer.

But Edrin was staring at Franz: staring at him and staring at him with eyes as green as the tree tops. The intensity of her hawk-sharp gaze wrapped round him so tightly that for a moment it was hard to breathe.

And Franz, with a shiver of dismay and excitement, could almost feel the talons holding him fast.

HISTORICAL NOTE

The night of 9/10 November 1938, when Nazi mobs attacked Jewish people, homes, and synagogues has become known as *Kristallnacht* (Crystal Night) because of the huge number of windows broken.

The Nazis claimed to base many of their policies on the science of evolution. Unfortunately the Nazis were very poor scientists, as well as being vile human beings. Their rule led to many millions of deaths amongst the disabled, Gypsies, homosexuals, Jews, Slavs, soldiers and civilians both before and during the Second World War.

The demon pits on the common were dug during the *First* World War as trench-building practice. They still exist, as a memento of a different human folly.

Tribe music is stolen from the stars, but the words of their songs are stolen from demons. The two Tribe songs in this book are known amongst demons as *The Hunting of the Cheviot* and *Tam Lin*.

ACKNOWLEDGEMENTS

Many thanks to Stefanie Logie, who so kindly and entertainingly answered all my questions about life in Berlin in the 1930s.

If I asked the wrong questions, or got her answers inside out, then it is, of course, entirely my own fault.

Tom had never been to
the city of the demons
before, and it smelt of
death. He stood and
shivered by the bridge
over the river, his skin
prickling with danger.
It was madness to cross—
but then he was in danger
if he stayed, too.

Cold Tom

Sally Prue

'One of those rare, strange, wonderful books that makes you see the world through different eyes' GUARDIAN

Tom is one of the Tribe. But he is not like the others—he is
clumsy and heavy, and the Tribe drive him away into the demon
city. But Tom can't live with demons either—they are so hot, so
foul, and he knows they are trying to enslave his mind.

But there is nowhere else to run. Between the savage Tribe
and the stifling demons, is there any way out for Tom?

'outstanding'
THE SUNDAY TIMES

SALLY PRUE

Wheels of War

In a country that's at war, anyone can be a hero ...

England, 1822

At first the war seems very far away. The King's men are so splendid in their scarlet coats, and they are fighting so bravely against the rebels, that it seems impossible that Will could ever leave his place in the big house with the Master and the womenfolk to have anything to do with the fighting. Will is too young, and too simple, and the war is too valiant and glorious for the likes of him.

But wars do not always keep their distance, and there is more than one way of being brave ...